'You have absolutely *no* right to interfere in my life!'

Xavier informed Louisa smoothly, 'Since you are my future wife, you should be under the close chaperonage of my aunt.'

'*I don't believe it!* And don't waste your breath on any more nonsense about your "honour" — because I think the whole concept is ridiculous!'

'Nevertheless, it's the only course open to someone, such as myself, who believes in and reveres the traditions of their homeland.'

Dear Reader

Bondiornu! Welcome to Corsica, the 'scented isle' where Napoléon was born, 'the nearest of the faraway islands', where spectacular mountains form a backdrop to a wide variety of coastal resorts. A holiday in Corsica could be both simple and sophisticated, either tranquil or action-filled — who could ask for more? So sit back and let Mary Lyons' new addition to our Euromance series whisk you away. *A vedechi!*

The Editor

The author says:

'I can't decide what it is about Corsica which haunts the memory and calls one back, time and again, to this staggeringly beautiful island. Is it the long, golden sandy beaches only a few kilometres away from soaring mountain peaks? Or the fierce passion and drama of Corsica's turbulent past? Do go and see for yourself. Maybe *you* can discover the secret of this enchanting and magical island.'

Mary Lyons

★ TURN TO THE BACK PAGES OF THIS BOOK FOR *WELCOME TO EUROPE*. . .OUR FASCINATING FACT-FILE ★

LOVE'S REVENGE

BY
MARY LYONS

MILLS & BOON LIMITED
ETON HOUSE, 18–24 PARADISE ROAD
RICHMOND, SURREY, TW9 1SR

*First published in Great Britain 1993
by Mills & Boon Limited*

© Mary Lyons 1993

*Australian copyright 1993
Philippine copyright 1994
This edition 1994*

ISBN 0 263 78357 X

*Set in 10 on 10 pt Linotron Times
01-9401-63126*

*Typeset in Great Britain by Centracet, Cambridge
Made and printed in Great Britain*

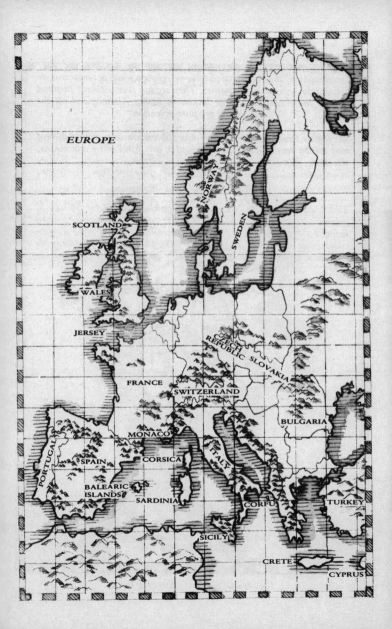

CHAPTER ONE

'I AM, of course, quite accustomed to being chased by women — even if they are seldom as beautiful as yourself, *mademoiselle*! However, I regret to have to say that you are wasting your time — and mine.'

Louisa Thomas barely registered the arrogantly drawled words. She could only stare in bewilderment at the tall, broad-shouldered figure sitting behind a large desk on the far side of the room.

Closing her eyes for a moment, Louisa struggled to clear her dazed and weary mind. Since catching the ferry from Nice to Corsica late last night she'd barely had a wink of sleep. So, maybe she was hallucinating? But when she opened her eyes again, it was to discover that she *hadn't* been mistaken. Instead of the elderly, silver-haired aristocrat whom she'd been expecting to see, Louisa now found herself gazing at a tall, dark and strikingly handsome man. A man who was, she realised with increasing dismay, quite clearly not a *day* over thirty-five years of age!

'I am still waiting to hear your explanation for this intrusion, *mademoiselle?*'

'I'm sorry,' Louisa gulped nervously, making a determined effort to pull herself together. 'I'm afraid that I've obviously made a mistake. The fact is. . .I was. . . well, I was hoping to meet a Comte Cinarchesi,' she muttered breathlessly, casting a quick, apprehensive glance about the large office. 'But, maybe your father. . .?'

'My father has been dead for many years,' the man informed her brusquely, rising from his chair and walking slowly around the desk. 'And you are not mistaken — I am indeed Comte Cinarchesi.'

'But. . .but you *can't* be!' she exclaimed helplessly, completely unable to accept the fact that this tall, elegant and outstandingly handsome figure could poss-

7

ibly be the grim 'wicked uncle' who was apparently determined to wreck her stepbrother's life.

As a rising young executive of a prestigious estate agency in London, specialising in the development of luxury homes in Europe, Louisa had met many handsome men. But never, she told herself as she tried to clear her dazed mind, *never* anyone as stunningly good-looking as this man. His loose curly hair, the blue-black colour of raven's wings, tumbled casually over the wide forehead of a tanned, hawk-like face which appeared to be stamped with the ingrained marks of centuries of breeding. There was a rakish, devil-may-care curve to his lips and with large, dark, glittering eyes set beneath thickly arched black brows he appeared to be the living embodiment of every woman's dream hero.

No wonder he'd so arrogantly accused her of 'chasing' him! Louisa hadn't a moment's doubt that ever since he'd grown out of short trousers this man must have been fighting off the women — in droves!

'I can assure you that I *am* Comte Cinarchesi!' the man told her firmly as he perched casually on the edge of the large desk, clearly regarding her obvious confusion with sardonic amusement.

Oh, lord! Her stepbrother, Jamie, must have got hold of the wrong surname! How *could* he have made such a dreadful error? Louisa bit her lip, staring blindly down at the thick carpet. Of course, it certainly wouldn't be the first occasion that Jamie Kendall's hopelessly casual, lackadaisical approach to life had led to muddle and confusion. Only *this* time it was beginning to look as if he'd really landed her in the soup! And how she was going to extricate herself from such an awful, embarrassing situation, she had absolutely *no* idea.

Now — when it was far too late — Louisa realised that on receiving Jamie's panic-stricken phone call from London last week she ought to have known that it would lead to dire trouble. But her stepbrother had sounded so desperate — especially at the thought of losing both his fiancée and his new job — that she'd weakly agreed to do what she could for him during her forthcoming brief visit to Corsica.

'OK—OK,' she had sighed with resignation. 'But I'm working flat out down here in the South of France for at least another week. In fact, I'm only going to be spending a day or two in Corsica—closing a deal on some development land—before heading straight back to London. So it really would be far better if *you* sorted out your own problems by getting in touch with this Comte Cinarchesi straight away.'

But her sensible advice had fallen on deaf ears. Clearly terrified of having any contact with the man, who was apparently threatening to ruin his life, her stepbrother had tearfully begged for Louisa's help.

But now, as she desperately tried to think of a reasonable explanation for being here in Comte Cinarchesi's office, Louisa could cheerfully have strangled her young stepbrother. Only Jamie could have been so stupid as to become involved with a young French girl just a few weeks after becoming engaged to marry the daughter of his new boss, Lord Armstrong. And even if her stepbrother now bitterly regretted his brief fling—mostly the result of a lovers' quarrel with his new fiancée—it was typical of Jamie's bad luck that the French girl should turn out to have a fiercely protective, rich Corsican uncle, who was apparently breathing fire and vengeance.

Unfortunately, it was also typical of Jamie's incompetent grip on life that he'd apparently given her the wrong name. The very idea of this rivetingly attractive man being the elderly 'wicked uncle' of whom her stepbrother was so afraid was *totally* ridiculous!

'Come, *mademoiselle*—let us have no more of this nonsense!' The Comte's harsh, sardonic voice broke into her distraught thoughts. 'May I remind you that I am *still* waiting to hear why it is you wish to see me?'

Louisa raised bemused, dazed eyes towards the tall figure lounging casually against the desk. On discovering her nationality he had, with typical continental politeness, immediately switched to speaking faultless English. Unfortunately, despite his total command of her native language, the Comte's low, deep voice and his sexy French accent seemed to be affecting her in an acutely disturbing manner.

She felt. . .well, she was definitely feeling *very* peculiar. It was as if a mass of fluttering butterflies had suddenly taken possession of her stomach. Maybe it was due to the silence in this large and luxurious office, or possibly the constrained and tense atmosphere caused by her sudden appearance in his private domain, but Louisa suddenly found herself desperately wishing that she was a million miles away from the presence of this disconcerting man.

Although why she should find him quite so intimidating, she had absolutely no idea.

Despite the fact that the Comte appeared to be wearing rather plain clothes, Louisa had already noted his handmade silk shirt, Hermès tie and the fact that his soft wool and cashmere hand-tailored dark suit was complemented by black leather shoes from a famous Florentine shoemaker. With the discreet glint of diamonds studding the thin gold watch on his wrist, and a heavy gold signet ring set with a large emerald on his little finger, everything about Comte Cinarchesi shrieked of wealth and privilege.

Thanks to her job, she was well used to mixing with the very rich. And, since his obvious affluence held no terrors for her, she couldn't think of a reasonable explanation for why she should feel so unaccountably nervous of this man. Could it be his air of careless arrogance, which seemed to proclaim that it mattered not a jot to him what other, lesser mortals might think, that he was a man who lived only by rules of his own making? If so, that would mean that he could be a very dangerous man to cross—and possibly *that* was why she was aware of loud and strident alarm bells ringing so noisily in her tired brain.

The Comte frowned, gazing across the room at the girl who was continuing to stare at him in silence.

Quite *why* he should be sitting here, patiently waiting for her to find her tongue, he had no idea. Especially since his taste usually ran to petite women with hourglass figures. Surely it couldn't be that he was attracted to this tall, slim and dramatic-looking female, with a cloud of red-gold hair tumbling about her shoulders? Although there *was* something strangely appealing about the English girl gazing at him with such startled, emerald-green eyes. She reminded him of a finely bred racehorse, nervously poised as if for instant flight.

'My patience is coming to an end, *mademoiselle*,' he told her with a shrug of his broad shoulders. 'Unless you are willing to tell me what you want, I think that it is time you left. Don't you?'

'Yes. . .yes, I mustn't take any more of your valuable time,' Louisa agreed quickly.

Having spent a long and tiring day fruitlessly tracking down — as it now turned out — completely the wrong man, she couldn't wait to get back to her hotel and have a long, cool shower. In fact, after all these years of keeping a wary and protective eye on her charming but somewhat wild stepbrother, it really was about time that he learned to sort out his own problems. This stranger, Comte Cinarchesi, had been remarkably patient in the circumstances, and clearly the sooner that she got out of here, the better.

Thinking about the matter later, Louisa could only come to the conclusion that it must have been the strange, glittering light in the Comte's dark eyes which had made her feel so unaccountably nervous as she backed away towards the door. But undoubtedly *something* must have lain behind the fact that she seemed to have lost her normal cool, calm grip on life. Why else should she have found herself babbling like an idiot, 'I'm sorry to have bothered you. . . A stupid mistake. . . You couldn't possibly be an uncle of a young, eighteen-year-old girl!'

The Comte's curt reply that yes, indeed he was, abruptly halted her progress towards the door.

Feeling as though she'd been suddenly hit by a heavy sandbag, Louisa stared at him with stunned eyes. 'Er — I don't suppose. . .? Her name wouldn't be Marie-Thérèse, would it?'

Her hesitant, tentative question seemed to have a

dramatic effect on the Comte. His dark brows drew together in a deep frown, his whole bearing and manner appearing to change in the twinkling of an ey1. From lounging casually against the desk, and regarding her with some considerable amusement, his tall figure was now stiff and very still, as he regarded her with a blank, mask-like expression.

'I would be interested to know exactly *why* you are interested in my niece,' he demanded, the cold, icy note in his voice sending shivers down her backbone.

With her mind in a total whirl, Louisa tried to persuade herself that it was *just* possible that she and this man could be dealing with a totally amazing coincidence. But, in her heart of hearts, she knew that she was about to discover that such accidents of fate only occurred in books, and never in real life.

'I can assure you that I've never met your niece,' she assured him quickly. 'In fact, the only reason why I'm here to see you is that I'm acting on behalf of my stepbrother, James Kendall. He apparently met this young girl, Marie-Thérèse Moncourt, when she was on holiday in London, and ——'

The Comte's harsh snort of contempt cut brutally across her words. 'And where *is* Monsieur Kendall?' he demanded.

'Well, he's very busy; and can't leave his work at the moment. So he asked me ——'

'*Hah*! I might have known that he is the sort of man who hides behind another woman's skirts!' the Comte ground out, his voice hatefully insulting as he walked slowly and menacingly towards her, like a panther intent on stalking his prey.

'Jamie is *not* hiding behind my skirts!' she retorted, before realising that there was a good deal of truth in the Comte's accusation. Strangely, this only served to increase her anger with the man who had now come to a halt, his tall frame looming over her. 'It's just. . . well, my stepbrother has just started a new job. So it's very difficult for him to take time off work.'

'A puerile excuse!'

'I'm telling you the truth!' Louisa protested.

'Really?' the Comte drawled, gazing scornfully down the length of his aristocratic nose, his wide, thin lips twisted with contempt.

Louisa glared up at him, only just managing to suppress an almost overwhelming urge to slap the supercilious smile off his handsome face. Despite his drop-dead good looks, the Comte was obviously a deeply unpleasant and thoroughly obnoxious man.

'Let me tell you,' the Comte ground out, 'no true Corsican worth the name — or even a Frenchman, come to that — would dream of allowing a female relative to become involved in such an affair. It is, however, just what one would expect of the English, *n'est-ce pas*?'

'*N'est-ce pas* nothing!' she snapped back furiously. 'And you can forget any of that stupid, chauvinistic nonsense. We're all in the Common Market now — and don't you forget it!' she added through clenched teeth, adding emphasis to her point by raising a finger and prodding him in the chest.

'Don't you *dare* touch me — you red-haired vixen!' he rasped, his hand snaking up to quickly grab hold of her wrist.

As she was trying to tug herself away from his fierce grip, her high heels seemed to catch in the carpet. Struggling to regain her balance, Louisa suddenly found herself jerked swiftly forward, hard up against the Comte's broad chest.

'Let go of me you. . .you damned Corsican!' she panted breathlessly. Determined to give him a piece of her mind, she made the mistake of raising her head to glare furiously at the man towering above her.

And clearly it *was* a mistake. Because, as she found her gaze caught and held by the gleam in the glittering dark eyes gazing so fiercely down at her, her brain seemed to become an empty void. She couldn't seem to think straight, or even to remember what it was she'd been going to say. In fact, the only stray thought which flickered across the blank tape running through her mind was surprise to discover that his glowing dark eyes were actually a deep navy blue flecked with gold, like lapis lazuli. As she gazed into their glittering depths, in some strange way it felt as if her whole existence was melting away, dissolving beneath the compelling light in those wide, piercing eyes.

A moment later she was jerked back to reality by the rasping sound of the Comte swearing violently beneath his breath as he pushed her quickly away.

While they stood glaring at one another in silence, Louisa found herself belatedly returning to earth with a thump. She could feel a deep flush creeping up over her pale cheeks, and it seemed to take the most tremendous effort to pull herself together, and to remember why she was here in this man's office.

Unfortunately, there seemed little she could do to prod her sluggish brain into some form of cohesive thought, especially when she tried to work out all the ramifications of the present situation. However, there definitely seemed no doubt that — impossible as it might be to believe — this man really *was* the uncle of whom Jamie had been so afraid.

According to her stepbrother, he and Marie-Thérèse had done little more than hold hands and exchange a few kisses. So Louisa hadn't been able to understand why the French girl's Corsican uncle — supposedly a massively rich international financier — should have become so incensed on hearing of his niece's brief flirtation, nor why he should have swiftly hauled the young girl off to his holiday home in Corsica. The whole story, as related by Jamie, had seemed very bizarre. In fact Louisa hadn't been entirely convinced by his alarming statement that he'd received a desperate phone call from Marie-Thérèse, who was being held virtually a prisoner in Comte Cinarchesi's ancient, mountain-top castle.

But now, with the Comte's dark glittering eyes boring into her own, Louisa had no difficulty in believing the whole weird story.

It looked as if Jamie had been quite right to be frightened of this man, she acknowledged shakily as she strove to regain her equilibrium. For her part, she'd rather be in a cage with live tigers than forced to deal with this extraordinarily fierce man. However, if she wanted to help her stepbrother, she had no alternative but to try and make her peace with the Comte.

'I. . . I don't think you quite understand the situation,' she began, her lashes fluttering nervously beneath his gaze as he continued to stare silently down at her. 'James Kendall is my stepbrother. And, since I was due to visit Corsica on business, he asked me to call and see you, in person.'

'I am touched by your sisterly concern,' the Comte drawled sarcastically. 'But nevertheless, it does not excuse your brother's absence. Clearly he is not man enough to face up to his responsibilities!'

'I'm sure that's not true!' she protested quickly. 'My brother tells me that you know about his fiancée. . . that he's just become engaged to Sonia Armstrong? He has also told me that apparently you've had business dealings with Sonia's father, Lord Armstrong.'

'You are quite correct; I have.'

'Well, in that case, I probably don't have to tell you that Lord Armstrong — the chairman of the merchant bank Armstrong Spencer — is not only an important and powerful man, but he's also well known for being a very difficult, hot-tempered personality.'

Louisa paused for a moment, but when the Comte merely continued to stare down at her she continued hesitantly, 'Surely you can see the problem facing my brother? He can't suddenly leave his job and fly down here to Corsica. Not without his fiancée and his boss, who also happens to be his future father-in-law, wanting to know what's going on?'

There was a long, tense pause before the Comte shrugged his broad shoulders and walked slowly back across the thick carpet, placing a small upright chair in front of the desk before resuming his own seat on the other side.

'Sit down,' he commanded, nodding curtly at the empty chair and impatiently drumming his fingers on the desk as she slowly obeyed his summons. 'While I admire your loyalty, I am still waiting to hear what your brother is intending to do about my niece, Marie-Thérèse.'

'I honestly don't see the problem,' Louisa sighed. 'Of course, it was quite wrong of Jamie to become involved with your niece when he was already engaged to marry someone else. However, it seems that Marie-Thérèse only stayed in London for one week, before returning to Paris. And my stepbrother has now made up the quarrel with his fiancée. So, as far as I'm concerned——' Louisa gave a tired shrug, '—I don't understand why you're making such a fuss about what is, quite clearly, an innocent friendship.'

'Innocent. . .?' The Comte gave a short bark of contemptuous laughter. 'There is nothing "innocent" about your brother's behaviour in this affair! There is no doubt that Marie-Thérèse has been gravely dishonoured—and therefore a wedding must be arranged as soon as possible.'

'A. . .a *wedding*? Between my brother and your niece. . .?' Louisa gave a strangled, hysterical laugh. 'Oh, come on! That's totally ridiculous!'

'Really? May I ask why you find it so amusing?' he drawled coldly.

'Because it's absolute nonsense—especially in this day and age—to take such a high-handed, outrageously moral view of a young couple's innocent friendship!'

'I cannot speak for what goes on in England, of course.' He waved his hand dismissively. 'But here, in Corsica, I can assure you that our traditional customs and culture are very important, that, of all the qualities a man can possess, his *honour* is of paramount importance.'

Louisa sighed and leaned back in her chair. It had been a long day, and she was very tired. Was there *no* way to make this man see sense? Was he *seriously* demanding a shot-gun marriage, simply because of a brief flirtation between Jamie and his niece? This whole affair was becoming more bizarre and ludicrous by the minute.

'I simply don't understand why you're making such a fuss about what is, quite clearly, a very trivial affair,' she muttered, brushing a weary hand through her cloud of red-gold hair.

The Comte swore briefly under his breath. 'There are many things that you do not appear to "understand", my dear Miss Kendall,' he growled impatiently.

Ignoring Louisa's attempts to explain that she bore a different surname from that of her stepbrother, he icily continued, 'You certainly don't appear to understand that you are now in Corsica. This island has a long and honourable history of fierce resistance to those who sought to impose their own cultures and customs upon us. But, despite now being a *département* of France — with all the undoubted advantages of being part of that strong, thriving republic — we Corsicans still retain our individual identity. So that, while we have turned our back on the past, and families on this island no longer slaughter each other simply because a man has tried to flirt with a virginal young sister or daughter, I can assure you that both I and any other red-blooded Corsican would seek justice for the fact that my niece has been clearly "dishonoured" by your brother!'

'You must be out of your mind!' Louisa exclaimed, leaping to her feet as she gazed at him with incredulous eyes.

'Oh, no — I can assure you that I am perfectly sane,' he retorted firmly.

'I've heard all about this island's history of revenge and bloody vengeance,' she informed him bluntly. 'But I can't believe that such things can happen nowadays! Not for something so simple as a man and a woman holding hands with each other, and maybe exchanging just a kiss or two. Surely the girl's parents——'

'Marie-Thérèse's parents are separated, and I am her legally appointed guardian,' the Comte informed her coldly.

'Well — what about your wife? Surely she must be able to take a more sensible view of this silly nonsense?'

'I have no wife.'

'*I'm not surprised!*' Louisa gave a snort of grim laughter as she continued to pace angrily up and down in front of the desk. 'I can't see *any* woman being desperate enough to marry a man with such crazy, old-fashioned ideas! Even if you are obviously as rich as Croesus,' she added spitefully.

The tightening of his lips, and a rising dark flush of colour beneath his skin, gave her a sense of fierce satisfaction. He was clearly furious at her suggestion that it was only his wealth which would lead women to find him attractive.

Unfortunately, she knew that it wasn't true. Louisa had no doubt that this man had merely to beckon with his little finger to have half the women in the world instantly placing themselves at his disposal! Not that she would be among their number, of course. *She—* thank goodness!—was completely immune to the outrageously sensual aura of the Comte's strong, sexual attraction. All the same. . .Louisa couldn't help wondering why he wasn't married. Especially since he was clearly such a dynamically vibrant male animal.

The Comte's harsh voice cut across her thoughts. 'I can well understand that Monsieur Kendall has spun you a fairy-story regarding his affair with my niece.' His voice was scathing and heavy with contempt. 'Unfortunately, Marie-Thérèse tells a very different story!'

His words pulled Louisa up short, acting like a dash of icy-cold water on the flames of her anger.

Could Jamie have been lying? she wondered, biting her lip as she stared silently back at the Comte. It wasn't impossible. In fact, if he was frightened enough, it was *very* possible that her stepbrother had not told her the full truth about his relationship with Marie-Thérèse.

Becoming quickly aware of her sudden doubt and confusion, the Comte rose from his chair, moving slowly and purposefully down the room towards her.

'I think it would be as well if you were to check your facts,' he told her in a clipped, hard voice as he came to a halt in front of her. 'It may well be that you are innocent in this matter. In fact, it occurs to me that you are being cynically used by your brother—in a shameful attempt to evade his clear responsibility towards my niece.'

'No!' she protested, valiantly trying to sound more certain than she felt.

'Your brother may not be capable of telling the truth,' the Comte spat, placing his hands firmly on her shoulders. 'But don't make the mistake of trying to lie to *me*!' he added with low, terrifying menace.

'I'm not lying!' she wailed helplessly, trying in vain to escape from his powerful grip. Her actions only served to increase the pressure of his fingers as they bit cruelly into her soft flesh.

'Look at me!' he commanded fiercely, pulling her struggling figure hard up against the length of his tall, firm body. 'Look at me — and then try and tell me the truth!'

Instinctively responding to the angrily rasped command, Louisa raised her head to gaze up into the fathomless depths of the gold-flecked, dark navy blue eyes staring down at her so intently. It suddenly felt as though the large room were shrinking to encompass their still figures, and she was aware of feeling almost sick and light-headed. Her senses reeled as his fingers relaxed their harsh grip, moving slowly down the line of her back, and pressing her even closer to him. Swirling darkness seemed to fill her dazed brain, and it was some time before she realised that the Comte appeared to be saying something to her.

'. . .feeling faint? When did you last have a meal?'

She stared uncomprehendingly up at him. It seemed to take the most enormous effort of will to even try and understand what he was saying. And then, as she slowly managed to pull herself together, Louisa was devastated to find herself clasped within the Comte's arms, with her head resting against the curve of his broad shoulder.

'When did you last have a meal — something to eat?' he repeated slowly, raising a hand to gently brush a stray tendril of red-gold hair from her brow.

It was the soft touch of his fingers on her flesh, sending shock-waves spiralling through her trembling body, which helped to dissolve the mist in her tired mind.

'I. . .I'm sorry, I can't think what's happening to me,' she muttered helplessly, her face flaming with embarrassment at being held so tightly within this man's embrace. How could she be behaving like this?

'I suspect that — somewhat unromantically, I'm afraid! — you are suffering from a lack of food,' he told her with a wry, sardonic twist to his lips. 'You should eat more. It seems to me that you are far too thin.'

As he spoke, his hands were soothingly caressing the long, lean lines of her slim body, the erotic warmth of his fingers slipping down over the vertebrae of her backbone, inducing a curious state of both languorous inertia, and an ever-increasing sense of heat flooding through her body. She wanted to stretch and purr like a cat in front of a warm fire.

As his dark tanned face seemed to swim before her vision she could only wonder, with the very small part of her brain which was still functioning normally, why she should have this feeling that she was being swept inexorably off her feet — feet which were normally so very firmly set on the ground.

The Comte gazed down at the girl, at the fluttering eyelashes over her wide, dazed green eyes, the flushed cheeks and the warm curve of her quivering lips.

'I think. . .yes, I think that I find you quite irresistible,' he murmured softly as he lowered his dark head slowly towards her.

Louisa's normally capable mind seemed to be shattering into tiny fragmented pieces, all whirling and swirling through her brain. He was. . .he really *was* going to kiss her! She had never found herself in a situation like this in all her life! She must do *something*! But it was too late. The hands which had been so gently caressing her were now tightening firmly about her trembling body, his mouth hotly demanding as it fastened on her lips.

For one shocked moment she froze, and then, as his kiss deepened, his warm tongue exploring the inner softness of her mouth, she found herself surrendering to the liquid fire coursing through her trembling body. Like a butterfly shedding its chrysalis, she found herself responding to this man's embrace as if she were a completely different person, inhabiting a strange and hitherto unknown planet.

What on earth was happening to her? What was this extraordinary sensual excitement which seemed to have hypnotised her senses? As she absorbed the warmth of his tanned cheek against hers and the intoxicating, musky scent of his cologne, the fierce and erotic clamouring of the blood in her veins flared into molten lava as he hungrily crushed her against his hard, muscled thighs.

And then there was no time for questions as Louisa found herself helplessly enmeshed, both by a force she hardly recognised, and one she couldn't possibly control. With a low moan she abandoned herself to her fate, raising her slim arms about his neck, her fingers burying themselves convulsively in his thick black curly hair.

Totally immersed beneath the deep waters of desire and passion, the two figures were abruptly brought back to reality by the sound of the office door being thrown loudly open.

'Well, well!' a low, husky voice exclaimed. 'It seems that I am interrupting a private tête-à-tête!'

With the harsh light of reality abruptly cutting through the thick mist of ardour in which she had been enmeshed, Louisa turned her dazed eyes on the female figure standing in the open doorway.

Small and petite, with a mass of coal-black, tightly curled hair tumbling about her shoulders, she was wearing a crimson silk dress which clung for dear life to her voluptuous hourglass figure. From the tip of her delicate nose, right down to the tiny feet encased in dainty, high-heeled sandals, she was perfect, exquisitely turned out — and one of the most beautiful women Louisa had ever seen. She also appeared to be very, *very* angry.

'Just *who* is this, *mon cher*?' she demanded of the Comte, her large dark eyes flicking contemptuously over the English girl's tall figure. 'I thought you were supposed to be taking *me* out to dinner this evening?'

'I fully intend to do so, Désirée,' he murmured. 'Unfortunately, this young lady is feeling a little faint,' he added, seemingly quite unperturbed at being discovered with his arms about a strange woman.

For her part, Louisa wasn't able to treat the embarrassing situation with anything like the same arrogant unconcern as the Comte. Almost overcome by the awkward, humiliating predicament in which she now found herself, she quickly tried to wriggle free of the arms still firmly clasped about her waist.

'This lady was feeling faint, you say?' The dark-haired woman, whom he'd addressed as Désirée, gave a caustic laugh, scrutinising Louisa with narrowed eyes and clearly not believing a word of what the Comte had said. Her suspicions were fuelled by the deep scarlet flush spreading across Louisa's cheeks. 'She does not look very pale to me!'

Managing at last to pull herself together, and realising that she was in no fit state to cope with this fraught and extremely tricky situation, Louisa determinedly brushed aside the Comte's arm.

'I—er—it's very late. . . I must go. . .' she muttered quickly, forcing herself to walk as swiftly as possible towards the door.

'Then we must not keep you,' Désirée agreed with a tight, malicious smile as she held the door open, ignoring the Comte's imperious demand for Miss Kendall to remain exactly where she was. '*Au revoir, chérie!*' the woman added, quickly slamming the door shut behind Louisa's trembling figure.

Luckily, a taxi was waiting outside in the street as she fled from the large office building. But, after jumping in and giving directions to the driver, she had little or no recollection of the journey back to her hotel. Forgetting why she had been there in the first place, forgetting all about her brother and his problems, her tired and weary brain was unable to think about anything except that extraordinary man, Comte Cinarchesi.

She was still finding it almost impossible to accept what had happened. Had she *really* been kissed by the frightening man? And how could she—who'd always prided herself on her good sense—have been behaving so *completely* out of character?

Leaning back in her seat, Louisa felt her cheeks burn at the recollection of just how enthusiastically and passionately she had returned the Comte's kisses. And trying to reassure herself that the brief episode would mean nothing to such an experienced man of the world didn't seem to help. Try as she might, there seemed nothing she could do to forget the amazing, devastating effect produced by the feel of his strong arms about her trembling body.

CHAPTER TWO

DESPERATELY exhausted, Louisa nevertheless found herself tossing and turning restlessly through the night, her fitful sleep dominated by the Comte's dark and handsome figure stalking arrogantly through her dreams.

When she woke up the next morning, although she was still feeling tired and sluggish, it was easier in the cold light of day to see her encounter with the fearsome Comte Cinarchesi in a more sensible, prosaic light. While she had obviously been tired and exhausted from her sleepless night on the ferry from Nice, she still couldn't understand her quite *extraordinary* reaction to the Comte. However, after bringing logic to bear on the problem, Louisa came to the conclusion that her temporary insanity *must* be due to the fact that she'd never had to deal with such an amazingly handsome and attractive man. He's wasting his time in that office, she thought sourly. Someone with that type of film-star looks could be earning a fortune in Hollywood!

Unfortunately, there was no way she could hide the fact that she'd behaved like a complete idiot. Goodness knows what it was about this beautiful, virtually unspoilt island, she was asking herself unhappily, when her dismal thoughts were sharply interrupted by the strident tones of a telephone ringing beside her bed. Brushing a tired hand through her sleep-tangled hair, Louisa grimaced as she realised there was only one person who could be calling her at such an early hour in the morning.

'What time are you meeting Xavier d'Erlanger?' a voice demanded impatiently in her ear.

'He's calling for me here, at the hotel, later on this morning,' Louisa said, muffling a sigh as she leaned back on the pillows, staring resignedly up at the ceiling.

It was absolutely typical of her boss, Neville Frost,

not to bother with any polite enquiries such as, 'Good morning' or 'Did you have a good journey?' As a director of Frost, Gerard and Lumley, the prestigious estate agency in London, Neville was determined to prove himself the equal of his grandfather, who'd been one of the original founders of the business. Ferociously ambitious, both for himself and the firm, he had swiftly expanded their business in Europe. 'The Common Market is a fact of life — and those who can't see the opportunities are either fools or totally braindead!' he'd pronounced at a board meeting some time ago, sweeping aside all opposition to his plans for large, upmarket housing and holiday developments in Spain, Italy, Portugal and the South of France.

'You and I are going places!' he'd announced, soon after she'd begun to work for him. And he was quite right — they had. In fact, Louisa had barely been able to catch her breath as he'd swiftly carved his way upwards through the firm, until Neville was now the senior partner and she, almost unable to believe her luck, not only had her own secretary and a department to run, but had now been put in sole charge of this important new development in Corsica.

'I don't expect there to be any slip-ups on this deal with Xavier d'Erlanger,' Neville was now telling her with hard impatience. 'It's a tough time for business nowadays, and I don't want the deal going sour on us. So make sure you're on the ball, right?' he added, a grim note of warning in his voice before he put down the phone.

'Thanks a bunch, Neville!' she muttered under her breath as she replaced her own receiver. She hadn't needed reminding of the particularly cut-throat business in which she was engaged, and Neville's implied threat that she was only as good as her last deal wasn't guaranteed to do anything for her self-confidence.

On the other hand, maybe she ought to be grateful that Neville hadn't asked too many searching questions. Because she was only too well aware that she should have spent the time since her arrival on this island yesterday finding out more about the background of the business financier Xavier d'Erlanger.

An incredibly rich worldwide financier, Monsieur d'Erlanger obviously believed in keeping a low profile. Despite all her efforts, Louisa had been unable to discover hardly anything about the mysterious Frenchman who, from his large office block in Paris, appeared to control many banks and financial institutions throughout the world. So what Xavier d'Erlanger was doing in Corsica, or why he was prepared to sell a large piece of land in the south of the island, she still had no idea. However, it was definitely a black mark for her to have failed to do her homework yesterday. And there was no way she could justify the hours she'd spent trying to track down and locate the awful Comte Cinarchesi. However, with her job now clearly on the line, Louisa knew that she couldn't afford to spend any more time on trying to sort out her stepbrother's problems.

All sense and reason told her that it was foolish to spend so much time worrying about Jamie. So why *did* she still feel so protective of the stepbrother who was only two years younger than herself? It had perhaps been understandable that she should want to care for the small, thin boy who'd been only ten years of age when his father had married her widowed mother. But she had become so used to rescuing Jamie from one dire scrape after another that it was only now, with this problem over Comte Cinarchesi's niece, that Louisa found herself taking a good hard look at their relationship.

Jamie had been only sixteen when both their parents had died, and maybe it had been a mistake for her to have taken on the role of a mother in his life. It was clearly time that she stopped trying to mollycoddle someone who was now a tall, good-looking man of twenty-three. In fact, as Louisa now guiltily acknowledged to herself, she'd been overwhelmingly relieved when Jamie had announced his engagement to Sonia Armstrong. A sensible and down-to-earth girl, Sonia had a cautious, matter-of-fact attitude to life which seemed to indicate that she was likely to be the perfect wife for Jamie. She and Louisa had already become very good friends, and that probably explained exactly *why*, against her better judgement, Louisa had agreed to try and sort out the problem of Comte Cinarchesi. However, there was clearly no hope of being able to reason with the fearsome man, nor any likelihood of sorting out the problems with the Comte's niece. So she could only be grateful that there was—thank goodness!—absolutely no danger of her ever having to meet him again.

It was a comforting philosophy, and one which helped her to face her breakfast of coffee and croissants, but which was fatally exploded by her phone call to Jamie.

Louisa had hoped that they would both be able to remain cool, calm and collected about the impossible task which he had set her. Unfortunately, all her good resolutions flew quickly out of the window only minutes after he had picked up the telephone in his flat in London.

'But why didn't you tell me the truth?' she demanded angrily after discovering that Jamie had, indeed, been lying, that he and Marie-Thérèse had indulged in a short, passionate affair. 'You quite clearly told me that you'd only held hands and exchanged a few kisses with the girl. Don't you understand what you've done?' she raged. 'The awful Comte clearly didn't believe a word I was saying. And now that I know the truth—I honestly can't say that I blame him!'

'But it wasn't *all* my fault, Lou,' Jamie protested weakly down the phone.

'Oh, no?' she snorted angrily. 'And who are you going to blame this time? Maybe Sonia—or me? Or possibly it was all due to a rush of blood to the head?' she added with heavy sarcasm.

'No—no, that's not what I meant,' her stepbrother protested. 'I was. . .well, I was just trying to say that it takes "two to tango".'

Louisa was definitely not in the mood to be amused. 'Two to—*what*?' she snapped.

'Oh, come on, Lou!' he sighed impatiently. 'If you want me to spell it out in words of one syllable — I can tell you that Marie-Thérèse certainly wasn't a virgin. As she said when we met, she was only interested in having a bit of fun, that's all,' he added, a strong note of grievance in his voice.

'That's *all*?' Louisa echoed incredulously. 'And what if the girl is now expecting a baby?'

Jamie's gasp of horror echoed loudly down the telephone line. 'You've got to be kidding!'

'Well, the Comte didn't exactly *say* that Marie-Thérèse was pregnant. But, now I come to think about it, that must be the reason behind his extra-ordinary demand that you and she should immediately get married.'

'*Married*. . .?' Jamie gave a shriek of anguish.

'Yes — I thought you might be interested to hear about that little item of news,' she told him grimly.

'Are you seriously saying. . .? Do you mean. . .?'

'The Comte claims that you have "dishonoured" his niece,' Louisa snapped. 'He's demanding an immediate marriage between you and Marie-Thérèse.'

'I don't believe it! Are you sure he isn't joking?' Jamie asked hopefully.

Louisa gave a short bark of angry laughter. 'I'm not sure about many things — but I am absolutely certain that Comte Cinarchesi is definitely *not* joking. And it sounds as though his niece must be pregnant,' she added harshly. 'Because it's the only reason that makes any sense of this whole ridiculous business.'

'Well, it might make sense to you — but it certainly doesn't to me,' Jamie retorted. 'And I can practically guarantee that Marie-Thérèse is *not* expecting a baby. She told me that she was on the Pill, and I also had the sense to take precautions myself. So I give you my word of honour, Lou, that there's no way the Comte can claim I am responsible for making that girl pregnant!'

'Don't talk to me about your "word of honour",' Louisa grated angrily down the phone, before once more reminding her stepbrother of his assurance that he had hardly touched the French girl.

'OK — OK. There's no need for you to take such a "holier than thou" attitude,' Jamie snapped back. 'What about you and Neville Frost? Or is it all right for you and Neville to have an affair, simply because he's your boss?'

'Neville and I are *not* having an affair,' she protested. 'It's just. . .well, we merely have an understanding — that's all.'

Louisa could feel her cheeks burning at the sound of her stepbrother's cynical laughter. It was no good. She'd given up trying to explain her relationship with Neville, since none of her female friends, nor her stepbrother, seemed able to understand that she and Neville were only good friends. They enjoyed working together and, when they did have an evening to spare from business, it was enjoyable to spend an hour or two quietly chatting over dinner. But, while Neville had made it clear that he was interested in a long-term friendship leading to marriage, that was as far as their relationship went, at present.

After all, as Louisa had so many times defensively reminded herself, she was still only twenty-five. And, although she had to admit privately that she and Neville seemed to have a somewhat lukewarm relationship, maybe that was why she'd never felt the urge to rush into marriage, especially when it involved making such an important commitment to another person, and requiring so much from them in return.

Jamie had accused her in the past of being super-cautious, claiming that by burying herself in work she couldn't hope to escape forever from the toils of love. But while she might occasionally feel restless, and was becoming increasingly aware that her present way of life didn't leave much time for romance, she still couldn't summon up much sympathy for her step-brother in his current predicament. And when he almost tearfully apologised for not telling her the truth, begging her to try and see Comte Cinarchesi again,

Louisa could only give a harsh bark of sardonic laughter.

'You must be *totally* out of your mind! There's no way I'm *ever* going anywhere near that man again! Although I've got to admit the Comte is quite right,' she added grimly. 'You should have taken leave of absence from your job, and been man enough to meet him face to face, here in Corsica.'

'*Please*, Lou——'

'No! Not only am I much too furious with you to discuss this matter any further, but I've also a very important business meeting this morning. So, since you've got yourself into this hole—I suggest you try and dig your own way out of it!' she added, angrily slamming down the phone.

Louisa glanced down at her watch, and gave a yelp of dismay. Thanks to Jamie and his problems, she was in grave danger of being late for her very important meeting with Xavier d'Erlanger. She must try to make a clear, determined effort to clear her mind of all the problems associated with her stepbrother. She was clearly going to need all her wits about her for the forthcoming negotiations, which, if they followed the usual pattern, were likely to be hard, tough and exhausting.

Normally relishing the exhilaration involved in a hard bargaining session, Louisa was finding it strangely difficult to work up any enthusiasm for the meeting which lay ahead. Even trying to come to a decision on what to wear was proving unusually difficult. Whether to put on trousers or a cool linen skirt seemed totally unimportant when her mind was still preoccupied with the traumatic events of last night. And suddenly re-alising that she hadn't told Jamie thatComte Cinarchesi was very far from being an ancient, crusty old man didn't help her concentration.

Eventually deciding that her visit to the site might include walking over rough terrain, Louisa slipped on a pair of navy blue linen trousers and a short-sleeved white linen blouse. Clasping a wide navy leather belt about her waist, she quickly checked her appearance in the mirror.

Did she look sufficiently businesslike? she wondered, grimacing as she tucked a stray lock of hair back into the knot on top of her head. Keeping her make-up to the minimum, she applied a pale pink lipstick to her mouth, which still felt bruised and swollen from the fierce pressure of the Comte's devastating kiss last night.

Not able to face the shame and embarrassment which had been momentarily reflected in her emerald-green eyes, she turned away to gather up a lightweight navy suede jacket, and, after checking through the contents of her blue shoulder-bag, she swiftly left the room.

Having some moments to spare before she was due to be collected by Monsieur d'Erlanger, Louisa was just glancing through a rack of postcards in the hotel lobby when she heard the receptionist call her name.

Walking across the heavy stone flags of the entrance hall, she suddenly felt as though she, too, had been turned to stone. Because there — standing at the reception desk only a few yards away — was the unmistakable sight of a familiar, tall figure.

Oh, *no*! If there was one person she had fervently hoped that she would *never* meet again, it was that quite awful Comte Cinarchesi! So what on earth was he doing here, at her hotel?

Half an hour later, as she gazed blindly out of the car window, Louisa was seething with frustrated rage and fury. She wasn't sure exactly *who* to blame for the predicament in which she now found herself. But she was quite certain, she told herself grimly, that she would have no trouble at all in cheerfully strangling either her brother, her London office — or that totally infuriating man, Comte Cinarchesi!

Casting a smouldering glance of anger at the tall, long-limbed figure sitting in the driving seat beside her, Louisa quickly turned her head to look back out of the window. She knew she ought to be admiring the picturesque scenery, as the long black Ferrari in which she was travelling snaked speedily along the twisting

road running south from Ajaccio. But she was just too
furious, both with the unfairness of life and with herself
for being such a blithering idiot, to fully appreciate the
lush green pastures, groves of eucalyptus trees, or the
fields bright with wild spring flowers which lined their
route.

When she had stood paralysed with fright back in
the foyer of her hotel, Louisa now knew that she ought
to have realised the truth—that the Comte would be
just as anxious as she was to avoid another fraught
encounter. But his tall, broad-shouldered figure,
clothed in a black leather jacket over slim black
trousers, had looked particularly frightening and sinis-
ter. After the embarrassing, exhausting scene last
night—not to mention the acrimonious telephone call
to her stepbrother—she'd naturally assumed that the
Comte had tracked her down to the hotel, fully intending to pursue his attempt to force Jamie to wed his
niece.

In total panic, and quite certain that she couldn't
face another confrontation with a man who scared her
half to death, Louisa had immediately tried to take
evasive action. Unfortunately, she just hadn't been
quick enough.

'Ah, *mademoiselle*. . .!' the young male receptionist
had called out as she was backing hastily away. 'This
gentleman wishes to see you,' he added, his loud voice
and beckoning hand making it impossible to ignore
him.

'No, you fool!' the Comte snapped. 'I certainly do
not wish to see this lady. I am here to meet a gentleman—a Monsieur Lou Thomas. It is possible that he is
an American,' the Comte added tersely, quickly grasping hold of the visitors' book and running his finger
impatiently down the list of names.

'But. . .but Your Excellency, I can assure you that I
speak the truth,' the receptionist protested. 'The only
guest by that name is now here before you.'

This can't be happening to me! Louisa told herself
with a muffled groan, briefly closing her eyes and
sending up a desperately fervent prayer for immediate

divine intervention. Unfortunately, no thunderbolt descended on either the Comte or herself, and she realised it was up to her to deal with this grimly farcical situation.

'I think you must be looking for me, since my name is Louisa Thomas. A fact which I could have told you last night, *if* I'd been given the opportunity to do so. But, unfortunately, as we both know—I wasn't!' she pointed out as coolly as she could. 'And in case you don't believe me, my passport is here, in the hotel safe.'

'Charming though you undoubtedly are, my dear *mademoiselle*, I'm afraid that I have no time this morning to pursue your delightful acquaintance,' the Comte drawled impatiently, his dark eyes flicking swiftly over the curves of her slim figure. 'However, if you would care to give my secretary a ring, I might be able to find time to take you out to dinner—possibly tonight?'

His sheer arrogance almost took her breath away! And while Louisa knew that she ought to be able to see the funny side of such an amazingly condescending statement, she discovered that she'd temporarily lost her sense of humour.

'I wouldn't have dinner with you—not even if you were the very *last* man on earth!' she retorted grimly.

Unfortunately, he did not appear to be listening as he reached inside his expensive leather jacket to remove a wallet, from which he extracted a folded piece of white paper. And as soon as she caught sight of the familiar letterhead, Louisa knew that she had been quite wrong in thinking that fate had no more nasty surprises in store for her.

'What on earth. . .?' she muttered, quickly seizing the paper from his hands. Ignoring the Comte's angry exclamation at her action, she quickly ran her eyes down its contents.

A faxed letter, written in French and dispatched from her London office some weeks ago, it confirmed her date of arrival and the hotel in which she was intending to stay. And it didn't take Louisa more than a few seconds to realise what had caused the confusion.

'There's your answer,' she told the Comte, putting the letter down on the desk and pointing to the relevant passage. 'What we are dealing with here is a simple typist's error. Where it should have said "Ms" Louisa Thomas, the girl in our London office has made a mistake in just typing "M." — the conventional way of writing "Monsieur" in French.'

'Thank you, *mademoiselle*, but I do *not* require a lecture from you on such matters,' the Comte drawled icily.

'Well, it seems that you do!' she told him grimly. 'Because I have to tell you, even though I'm sure you won't like it, that my colleagues will insist on calling me by the shortened form of my name, "Lou".'

'Do you seriously mean——'

'Yes,' she snapped impatiently. 'I keep telling you that my name *is* Louisa Thomas.'

For the first time since she'd met him, the Comte seemed to have lost a good deal of his sang-froid. In fact, the normally cool nonchalance and suave, sophisticated poise of the man appeared to be badly dented.

'But. . .but you are a *woman*!' he exclaimed, his voice rising with incredulity as he gazed at her in consternation. 'I really cannot be expected to do business with a female — and especially not one such as you!'

Louisa bristled. Once again, his arrogance was almost beyond belief.

'If the French Revolution was, as I understand, partly caused by the stupid, totally insensitive actions of the aristocracy, then it can only have been a good thing!' she ground out through clenched teeth.

But nothing, it seemed, could dent this man's amazing self-possession as he dismissed her words with a slight flick of his fingers, much as he would have brushed away a mildly annoying insect.

Louisa took a deep breath. 'OK, let's start again, shall we?' she said tersely. 'Like it or not, that letter is referring to me. And, if you have any doubts, I must tell you that Frost, Gerard and Lumley are my employers. However, *I* would like to know exactly how you have managed to get hold of Monsieur d'Erlanger's letter,' she demanded. 'I really cannot see what right you have to ——'

She was prevented from saying anything further as the Comte, swearing fiercely under his breath, quickly gripped hold of her arm. A moment later, Louisa found herself being hustled out of the hotel, and dragged roughly down the steps towards a long, low-slung black Ferrari standing at the kerb.

'I'm not going anywhere with you! And certainly *not* in that dangerous-looking vehicle,' she protested.

'Get in!' he growled, opening the passenger door.

'I demand to know what's going on,' she cried as he took a threatening step towards her.

'It may seem nothing to you, but I'm damned if I'm going to have my private business discussed — at considerable length — in front of a mere hotel receptionist,' the Comte ground out through clenched teeth. 'Now, are you going to get into my car?' he added menacingly. 'Or am I going to have to throw you in?'

The awful man was clearly deranged. But since he looked quite capable of putting his threat into action, Louisa merely scowled at him, before weakly doing as she was told. And by the time he had walked around the car, and was sitting down in the seat beside her, she was beginning to suspect the worst.

However extraordinary it might seem, it definitely looked as if Comte Cinarchesi and the international financier, Xavier d'Erlanger must be one and the same person!

'You're Monsieur d'Erlanger, aren't you?' she demanded as he fastened his seatbelt.

'Yes, of course.' He shrugged in a way that was totally Gallic as the powerful engine roared into life. 'I would have thought that fact must be obvious by now.'

'But why. . .?' She gazed at his tanned profile in bemusement. 'Why do you use two names? What are you — some sort of Jekyll and Hyde character?'

'Certainly not!' he retorted curtly, remaining silent

as he concentrated on driving through the narrow, crowded streets of the old town.

'The answer is, of course, a very simple one,' he said at last, clearly feeling able to relax his vigilance as they began to leave Ajaccio behind them. 'My family name is d'Erlanger, and I was a businessman in Paris for many years before I inherited the title of Comte Cinarchesi, from a great-uncle whom I'd never met. So for business purposes I still conduct my affairs under my given name of Xavier d'Erlanger. It is only here, in Corsica, that I use my title.'

'And I suppose it's just *my* bad luck that I had to meet both of you—at one and the same time!' Louisa ground out, almost choking with anger at the predicament in which she now found herself.

How on earth was she supposed to conduct a calm, civilised and yet hard-hitting negotiation over the price of some land which, it now turned out, was owned by the one man in the world that she'd have given her eye-teeth to avoid?

And that wasn't all, Louisa told herself gloomily. When conducting any business—especially with such an impossibly arrogant man like the Comte—she normally strove to keep her own private thoughts and opinions well away from the matter in hand. But now that Comte Cinarchesi, who'd kissed her so passionately last night, had suddenly assumed the mantle of the French financier, Monsieur Xavier d'Erlanger. . .? Well, she really didn't have a clue how she was going to handle what was obviously a *very* complicated situation!

'It is clearly pointless for us to be at odds with one another,' he said at last, his voice breaking into the long, tense silence within the vehicle. 'Unless and until I can make different arrangements, I suggest that we try to forget our romantic encounter last night. We must attempt to "bury the hatchet" as you say in England. Otherwise, it will be impossible for us to do business with one another.'

Louisa, staring glumly out of the window as they swept past the international airport, found herself reluctantly agreeing with the sense of what he said. Especially as it so clearly reflected her own thoughts on the matter. However, there was one question which had to be settled straight away.

'What am I supposed to call you? I mean. . .' She gave a helpless shrug, gesturing towards the car phone, attached to the dashboard. 'If someone calls you up on that machine—are they going to be talking to Comte Cinarchesi, or Monsieur d'Erlanger?'

Convinced that the man totally lacked a sense of humour, she was surprised to hear him give a short, rueful bark of laughter.

'It would seem, Louisa, that you and I have already gone far beyond mere *politesse*. So you may call me by my Christian name of Xavier, if you so wish. However,' he added coldly, 'when we are talking to one another in French, you do *not* have my permission to address me by the intimate form of the word "you".'

Louisa turned her head to glower at his handsomely tanned, hawk-like profile. She had always admired one of the conventions of the French language, which meant that one addressed ordinary friends and acquaintances as '*vous*', reserving the far more intimate '*tu*' for members of one's family, close friends—and lovers. Since she clearly did not come into *any* of those three categories, his crushing statement had been obviously designed to put her firmly and contemptuously in her place!

'That last remark of yours was totally unnecessary!' she snapped irritably. 'Especially since we are talking in English, and——'

'No. I have decided that from now on we will use *my* native tongue. I find it very boring to be forced to speak English. And besides,' he added in a condescending drawl, 'it is clear that you need to improve your very inadequate grasp of the French language.'

Arrogant swine! Gritting her teeth, Louisa struggled to control an almost overwhelming urge to scream out loud with frustration.

Her French wasn't *that* bad! In fact she'd had no difficulty at all in being understood during her recent

business trip to the South of France. However, if
Xavier was like most Parisians—who spoke very fast,
with little or no patience for those who weren't totally
fluent in their language—it was going to add a further
burden for her during their forthcoming negotiations.
There was always a certain amount of 'game playing'
when trying to arrange a deal. And it looked as if
Xavier meant to make sure that he held as many
winning cards as possible!

From almost the first moment she'd set foot on this
island, her visit had been clearly doomed to be one of
complete disaster! She should *never* have made the
mistake of coming to Corsica, Louisa told herself
miserably, staring out of the car window at the fragrant
groves of eucalyptus trees, which slowly gave way to
darkly forested slopes as the fast sports car sped along
the road towards the mountains ahead.

However, with Xavier remaining silent, clearly concentrating on the dangerous twists and turns of the
road as they climbed steadily upwards through a thick
forest of dark green pine trees, Louisa slowly began to
calm down. The charming view of tiny villages clinging
to the sides of the mountain, and the sight of romantic
old ruined castles, perched on granite crags high above
the road, seemed to act as a soothing balm on her
troubled spirits.

Despite the disastrous start to her visit, she was
quickly coming to the conclusion that Corsica, with its
highly dramatic scenery, was one of the most beautiful
islands she'd ever seen. And now that she was feeling
in a slightly more peaceful frame of mind, Louisa also
had to acknowledge that Xavier had been quite right,
there was absolutely no point in them quarrelling with
one another. While it was obviously impossible for her
to forget what had happened last night, she had to try
and dismiss it from her mind.

Not that she had any illusions about the man, of
course. He seemed to have a ridiculously old-fashioned
view of women—especially those engaged in business
affairs. And while she'd never had any sympathy with
the feminist cause, she couldn't help thinking that any

prolonged dealings with Xavier d'Erlanger could well
help to change her mind!

However, by the time they were descending through
the pine forest, towards a large village set in a valley
surrounded by a thick wood of tall chestnut trees,
Louisa found herself prepared to agree with Xavier's
suggestion that they should stop for a cup of coffee.
And he really did seem determined to keep his side of
the bargain. Confining his conversation solely to various aspects of Corsica's long history, and background
information on the island's most famous inhabitant,
Napoléon Bonaparte, she was feeling far more relaxed
by the time they were sitting at a table beneath
flowering trees in a courtyard behind the small café.

'I find it all very confusing,' Louisa admitted, savouring the soft, pine-scented breeze as she sipped her
strong dark coffee. 'Here we are, on a French island,
and yet it all seems so. . .well, so very Italian!'

'It is not so extraordinary, especially when you
realise that this island was ruled by Italy until only a
year before Napoléon's birth,' Xavier pointed out. 'In
fact I believe he spoke nothing but Italian, until he was
sent to be educated in France at nine years of age.'

'But how extraordinary that such a man should have
ended up as Emperor of France!' she said. 'The Corsican
people must be very proud of such a famous man.'

'Well — no, not entirely,' Xavier drawled wryly. 'The
fact is that after leaving the island Napoléon only
returned here once or twice for brief visits, and did
virtually nothing to improve the status or the dire
poverty of most of the inhabitants. So, as you can
imagine, the islanders have certain mixed feelings
about him.'

'But I've seen his enormous statue in the Place
General de Gaulle. And the guidebook to this island,
which I purchased in France, seems full of other old
buildings connected to the Bonaparte family,' she
protested.

Xavier shrugged. 'Ah, yes, but that is mainly for our
seasonal visitors, since tourism is the single largest
source of income on this island. All the same —' he

gave her a wolfish grin as he leaned casually back in his chair '—maybe I am being unfair to Napoléon, hmm? He did, after all, very nearly beat the British at Waterloo!'

Louisa laughed, by now feeling far too relaxed and good-humoured to be drawn into any more arguments with this difficult man.

'Indeed he did!' she agreed. 'Incidentally, did you know that Napoléon also called us "a nation of shop-keepers"? I think he meant it as an insult,' she added with a grin. 'Unfortunately, I'm sorry to say that it must have backfired on him, because the British have always taken that remark as a great compliment!'

Xavier laughed as he stood up to pay the bill. 'Yes, you are quite right. It seems there is definitely more than the Channel dividing our two nations.'

Since the smile accompanying his words was a remarkably warm and friendly one, Louisa found her-self returning to the car in a far better frame of mind than when she had left it. And it wasn't until they were well on the way to their destination, a site not far from the seaside town of Propriano, that she became aware that maybe prolonged exposure to this man—especially within the close confines of this narrow sports car—might not be a good idea.

It was difficult to work out exactly where the problem lay. It certainly wasn't that he had been trying to either flirt with her, or been guilty of making any suggestive remarks—because he most certainly hadn't. But there was no doubt that the extraordinarily strong, heady aura of sexual vigour which surrounded his tall figure—barely a few inches away from her own body—was having a most peculiar effect on her nervous system. There seemed no other explanation to account for the return of the uncomfortable sensation of butterflies fluttering madly in her stomach, nor for the shivering tremors which flicked across her skin each time he brushed casually and accidentally against her bare arm.

Quite honestly, she told herself wildly, if she didn't conclude this business as quickly as possible, and fly swiftly back to the safety and sanctuary of her own flat in London, she might well be in grave danger of making an utter fool of herself.

Although she didn't even like the man and he himself could barely seem to treat her with anything but icy politeness or contempt, she nevertheless seemed to be quite insanely drawn towards his dark, sensual attraction. And telling herself that she must be totally out of her mind didn't seem to make a blind bit of difference!

CHAPTER THREE

MAKING a determined effort to ignore Xavier's dark, disturbing presence, Louisa tried to concentrate on the passing scenery. Climbing up once more through the mountains, they now seemed to be descending through the foothills towards open pasture land. The banks of the streams and meadows were bright with spring flowers, and light blue splashes of wild lavender filled the landscape, a colourful contrast to the silvery leaves of the olive trees and the green fields, in which cows were munching the fresh spring grass.

Corsica was clearly a beautiful island. And Louisa could see that the picturesque scenery, visible wherever one turned, would prove to be a very strong point when drawing up a prospectus for any future development here.

In fact it was about time that she concentrated on her career. It would be disastrous to allow herself to be distracted from her job by Xavier. So far, his attitude towards her had been mainly a mixture of arrogance and contempt. But she had no doubt — as he had demonstrated so clearly last night — that he was perfectly capable of turning on the heavy Gallic charm if it suited him to do so.

It was extremely unlikely that Xavier had become a very successful and wealthy financier without using all the weapons at his command, Louisa warned herself grimly. She had important business to conduct, and the thought of Neville Frost's annoyance if she didn't achieve a favourable result helped to stiffen her resolve as they approached their destination.

The port of Propriano had, according to Xavier, been in existence since at least the second century before Christ.

'The Greeks, Romans and Carthaginians all occupied this area at one time or another,' he told her,

42

driving slowly through the town down to the port. 'Not to mention the Turkish pirates!' he added, telling her that even as late as the eighteenth century the raiding hordes of pirates had caused devastation in the small town.

Nowadays, however, things were very different, Louisa realised, looking about her with interest as Xavier brought the car to a halt near a large marina. Getting out of the car to admire the view across the wide sparkling expanse of the Gulf of Valinco, she could see that the port and town looked both busy and prosperous. Glancing to her right, she could see the strong midday sun sparkling off the steel balconies of the large white concrete hotels and blocks of apartments situated at the northern end of the town.

Since her company prided itself on employing architects whose brief was to provide designs which blended into the local landscapes, she was relieved to discover that the land he was selling lay to the south of the town, some distance away.

'I, too, do not care for large blocks of concrete,' Xavier agreed, when she made the point that Frost, Gerard and Lumley's development would be very different from the already established modern hotels. 'In fact,' he added as they returned to the car, 'it is because I visited a holiday complex built by your company, at Saint Raphaël in the South of France, that I agreed to sell my land to your firm.'

Louisa couldn't help feeling a small glow of satisfaction, since it was she who had overseen that particular development. Maybe these negotiations were going to work out all right, after all?

As they left the town, with Xavier pointing out the advantages of the local Tavaria Airport, she became confused at the inland route they seemed to be taking until, as the road slowly became little more than a track, she realised that they had completed a semi-circle, and were once more heading towards the sea. When he eventually brought the car to a halt, it was difficult for Louisa not to show too much enthusiasm, since it was immediately obvious that the area was just about perfect.

Surrounded by gently rolling hills, she found herself gazing down at the wide curves of a bay encircling a deserted beach of very fine, pale sand. There was an attractive small fishing port not far away, and with its spectacular views she needed no convincing that, suitably and carefully developed, any houses on this site would virtually sell themselves.

'Well?' Xavier murmured. Leaning casually against the bonnet of his car, he gazed at the tendrils of red-gold hair, whipped by the stiff sea breeze into a shining halo about the girl's pale face. 'What do you think?'

She gave a careless shrug of her shoulders. 'It's not too bad — I've certainly seen worse sites,' she told him, deliberately injecting a lack of enthusiasm into her voice. 'However, I'm not very happy about what looks like a steep climb down to the beach, or the force of this wind. If this part of the coast catches the *mistral*, it could prove to be a problem.'

'Nonsense! It only passes over the north-west of the island,' he protested, before checking himself with a wry laugh. 'Ah, I see that not only have you done your homework, Louisa — but that you are already starting to bargain with me!'

'Not at all.' She shrugged again. 'I was merely pointing out some obvious defects.'

Xavier raised a dark, sardonic eyebrow. 'It takes two to negotiate, and I do not intend to begin until after lunch,' he said, moving to the back of the low-slung sports car and unlocking the boot, before removing a wicker hamper and a tartan rug.

'As you can see,' he pointed out smoothly, some time later, 'it will be very easy for your company to build their houses well away from any prevailing wind.'

Although she affected to take no notice of his remark, Louisa had to admit privately to herself that he was quite right.

Expecting to be taken down to the beach for their picnic, she had been surprised when he'd led her away from the sea, back along a small track leading to one of several small hollows in the landscape. After he had spread the rug out on a patch of green grass surrounded by evergreen shrubs, whose white flowers gave off a strong, heady perfume, she realised that they were totally sheltered from the strong wind, only the lightest of soft breezes wafting gently through her hair.

So much for *that* point of debate! she thought ruefully, leaning back on her elbows and gazing up at the cloudless blue sky. Blushing as she saw Xavier's eyes flick over her breasts, which had been thrown into prominence by her action, she quickly sat up as he began to unpack the wicker basket.

'My goodness! I don't call this a picnic—it's more of a banquet!' she exclaimed in amazement.

Having expected the usual English fare of sandwiches and a Thermos of coffee, her eyes grew wide as she gazed down at the snowy-white linen napkins bearing a thick monogrammed crest, and the porcelain plates on which rested pots of *pâté de foie gras*, cold lobster in its shell, small chicken breasts wrapped in slivers of Parma ham, and fresh crusty rolls accompanying a large piece of creamy cheese. Her green eyes widened as Xavier also lifted a bottle of wine from the hamper, his brown tanned fingers deftly applying a corkscrew as he quickly removed the cork.

'Good heavens!' she breathed. 'We'll never be able to eat all that!'

Xavier gave her a quick smile, clearly amused at her surprise. 'After our climb up here—not to mention the strong bracing wind, about which you seemed so concerned!—I have no fears on that score.'

Once again, he proved to be quite right. The delicious food was totally irresistible. And when, some time later, he was pressing her to have some more of the delicious, locally made Roquefort cheese, she could only groan in dismay.

'Oh, no—I've already eaten *far* too much,' she protested as he poured her another glass of wine. 'I shan't be able to get into my clothes if I eat any more meals like this,' she added with a groan.

'I do not think there is any danger of that,' he

murmured, his dark eyes flicking over the soft curves
of her slim figure. 'Since you call yourself "Ms"
Thomas, may I ask whether you are married?'

'No — no, I'm not.'

'But surely you must have a boyfriend?' he enquired
smoothly.

'Yes — er — well, I suppose I do. Although it's more
of a good friendship, really,' she muttered with a slight
frown. 'Why do you ask?'

Xavier shrugged his broad shoulders. 'Not for any
particular reason,' he drawled. 'Although I must admit
it will be a new experience for me to conduct business
with a woman.'

'Oh, come on!' Louisa gave him an incredulous
smile. 'There must be many career women in Paris.'

'Yes, of course. But this situation is very different. I
do not normally find myself conducting business on site
with a beautiful and attractive woman. Especially not
one I have embraced only the day before with — how
shall I put it? — a certain amount of passion!'

Louisa could feel her cheeks blushing a deep, fiery
crimson beneath the gleam in his dark eyes. And the
low, sensual note in his voice wasn't doing anything for
her peace of mind, either. She was obviously going to
have to set the record straight, as quickly as possible.

'Thank you for the compliment, Xavier, but I
wouldn't like there to be any misunderstanding
between us,' she told him as coolly as she could. 'As
far as I'm concerned, I never mix business with
pleasure.'

'Never?'

'Absolutely *never*!' she repeated firmly, only to be
thrown into confusion as he gave a low, husky laugh.

'Well, it seems I must be content to know that you
regard my embrace as "pleasure". However, it is a pity
if, as you insist, I shall not have the equal pleasure of
once again tasting those soft lips. Or of feeling that soft
body trembling against my own, hmm?'

Oh, God! Louisa whimpered silently to herself,
desperately wishing that the earth would swallow her
up. Why did he have to keep going on and on about

their encounter yesterday? She'd never behaved like that with a strange man before—or with anyone else, for that matter. It seemed totally unnecessary for him to keep on referring to something of which she was *so* ashamed.

'I. . .I don't want to talk about it,' she muttered huskily, desperately avoiding his eyes as she stared fixedly down at the tartan rug. 'In fact, I would be grateful if we could keep the conversation strictly confined to our present business.'

'Very well,' he shrugged, beginning to pack the empty plates and napkins back in the wicker basket.

In the long silence that followed, Louisa desperately tried to think of a topic of conversation which would not lead up a dark alley, towards her utterly incomprehensible behaviour in his office. But it wasn't easy. Having done her best to forget the disastrous episode, his words had now brought back to the forefront of her memory all her shameful actions, her insane abandonment in the arms of a complete stranger.

Making a determined effort to try to pull herself together, Louisa tried to change the subject. 'Did—er—did you inherit this land from your uncle?'

'No,' he answered briefly, before giving another slight shrug of his shoulders. 'I bought it some nine or ten years ago, just before my marriage.'

Louisa frowned in puzzlement. 'I thought you said. . .well, I thought that you weren't married.'

'You're quite right, I'm not,' he agreed tersely, the expression on his tanned, handsome face becoming stern and forbidding as he gazed past her into the far distance. 'My wife was killed in a car accident, just a year after our wedding.'

Louisa regarded him with dismay. What on earth had prompted her to ask such a stupid question? From the sight of a pulse beating in his clenched jaw, it was clear that she had touched upon a raw nerve. And it was equally obvious that, even after all these years, Xavier was still unhappily mourning the loss of his wife.

'I'm so very sorry,' she said quickly, hastening to

make amends for her careless remark. 'I had no idea. . . I mean. . .'

'It all happened a long time ago.' He gave a brief, dismissive wave of his hand. 'As far as this land is concerned, I discovered it when visiting some distant cousins at Bonifacio, in the far south of this island. Since I was, at that time, just about to get married, it seemed a perfect place in which to build a large house for our summer vacations.'

Louisa nodded sympathetically. 'It is beautiful,' she agreed softly.

'Be careful, Louisa!' he drawled silkily, his dark eyes suddenly gleaming with sardonic amusement. 'Surely it cannot be either prudent or sensible for you to show your appreciation of this site? Particularly when you are clearly intending to drive a very hard bargain with me over the price!'

She shrugged. 'There's little to be gained in pretending that this is not an attractive site,' she told him, attempting to sound more business-like than she felt as she tried to muffle a tired yawn. 'But whether we can agree on a satisfactory price is quite another matter.'

Maybe it was the warm spring sunshine, or the effect of the wine which he'd so liberally poured into her glass, while consuming none himself. But despite urgently reminding herself to be wary of this dangerous man—especially if, as now, he wasn't behaving with his usual contemptuous arrogance—she found herself feeling slightly drowsy and very. . .well, *very* peculiar.

It was only a sudden, totally surprising urge to rest her dizzy head on his broad shoulder, and a curious longing to feel his strong arms about her body, that shocked her into sitting bolt upright. Ashamed to be even thinking such disgraceful thoughts, she desperately tried to clear her dazed mind.

'The question of a price for this land is, of course, the nub of the matter,' he agreed blandly. 'However, it seems to me that you are a little weary. Maybe you should have a brief rest?'

Taking absolutely no notice of her protests that she was feeling perfectly able to conduct business, Xavier

brusquely informed her that he would conduct negotiations in his own good time, before striding off down
the small track to where he had left his car.

Once again, the awful man was proving to be right,
Louisa wearily acknowledged as she lay back on the
tartan rug, relishing the warmth of the early afternoon
sunshine. Goodness knows what was happening to her.
Normally filled with boundless energy, she was completely at a loss to account for her overwhelming
feelings of drowsiness and exhaustion. She had hardly
slept at all last night, of course, but, even taking that
into account, as well as the two glasses of wine which
she had consumed, there seemed no reasonable explanation for her sense of overwhelming fatigue. Maybe if
she just closed her eyes for a few, brief minutes. . .

When she opened them again, it took her drowsy,
sluggish mind some moments to realise that she must
have fallen asleep. And even longer to come to the
conclusion that the handsome, tanned features filling
her glazed vision were not part of some erotic dream.

'I'm sorry. . .I can't think what happened. . .' she
muttered helplessly.

'You were clearly tired, and possibly affected by the
maquis,' Xavier told her, pressing her firmly back down
on to the rug as she struggled to sit up.

'The *maquis*. . .?' She frowned in bemusement,
before turning her head as he pointed to some white-
flowering shrubs, which were sited close to her and
whose heady, almost narcotic scent seemed to fill her
nostrils.

'It is practically our national flower,' he murmured,
explaining that the shrub was to be found throughout
the island, forming a dense jungle of aromatic evergreen plants which, in times gone by, had provided
cover and shelter for those Corsicans attempting to flee
and hide from the island's invaders.

Striving to pull her scattered wits together and to
concentrate on what he was saying, she noted that
Xavier was now reclining casually beside her on the
rug, his face and body only a few inches away from
her own.

Once again, like last night in his office, she couldn't seem to tear her gaze away from his face. It was as though she was drowning in the gleaming depths of his gold-flecked deep blue eyes. Her heightened senses were suddenly aware of the sharp, fragrant tang of his cologne and the thickly fringed length of his black eyelashes, the only feminine aspect of this fiercely masculine man. He was so close that she could see the faint, dark shadow along his strong jaw, betraying the fact that he might find it necessary to shave both night and morning, and there was little she could do to prevent a flush from staining her cheeks at the direction her thoughts were taking.

'Are you feeling all right?' he frowned, placing a cool hand on her heated forehead. And once again, like last night, the touch of his fingers on her skin seemed to spark off an explosion of nervous tremors, deep in the pit of her stomach.

'I—er—I can't stay here. I must get up,' she gasped breathlessly as he leaned closer to her supine figure.

'There is no need for hurry,' he murmured, lowering his body down towards her. She could feel his breath on her face, the steady thud and beat of his heart, so different from her own, which seemed to be racing out of control, a painful lump obstructing her throat.

'Please, Xavier!' she gasped helplessly as he pulled the combs from her hair and brushed his firm mouth across her soft lips. 'We mustn't. . . This is madness. . .' she managed to protest before his mouth closed firmly over hers, producing a shattering response that sent shock waves spiralling through her body.

She was drowning, sinking lower and lower into some dark void. A deep flame flared into pulsating life as she helplessly responded to the sensual mastery of his kiss. She couldn't prevent herself from giving a faint, low moan as his mouth left hers, and he trailed his lips down over her jaw to seek the hollow at the base of her throat.

Oh, lord! What was happening to her? 'Please—let me go!' she moaned, feeling a ridiculous sense of loss and deprivation as he bowed to her entreaty.

'There is no need to sound quite so dramatic,' he drawled sardonically, getting to his feet and gazing down at the clearly dazed, bemused figure of the girl. 'It was only a kiss.'

'There are kisses — and kisses!' she muttered grimly, trying to stop her hands from shaking with tension as she hurriedly replaced the combs in her hair. 'I thought . . .well, I'm sure that we'd agreed about the — er — importance of keeping our relationship on a professional level,' she reminded him as firmly as she could, while scrambling awkwardly to her feet.

Unfortunately, she was well aware that her attempts to sound confident and businesslike didn't seem to carry much conviction. But there was little she could do to prevent her body from still trembling with nervous reaction to his kiss. It might have meant nothing to him — but it had left *her* feeling totally devastated!

'You no longer need to have any fear about mixing business and pleasure,' he drawled with a cool, ironic smile. 'I have just been on the telephone to your London office, requesting that you be taken off this job. I have issued instructions for someone else to be sent over to deal with me in this matter.'

'You've done *what*?' she cried, staring at him in stunned outrage and dawning horror. 'That's absolute nonsense! I'm *perfectly* capable of dealing with this business. You. . .you simply *can't* do this to me!'

Xavier shrugged his shoulders. 'It is already done,' he drawled succinctly. 'And, as far as I'm concerned, there will be no further discussion on the subject.'

In a state of complete and utter shock, Louisa trudged silently behind Xavier's tall figure, back to where he had parked the car near the edge of the cliff, overlooking the wide, curving bay of Valinco.

She still hadn't managed fully to come to terms with or be able to comprehend the full extent of his duplicity: that of kissing her one minute — and then sacking her the next. It was only when he was replacing the hamper in the boot of the car, and was holding open the passenger car door, that the full enormity of his totally irrational decision finally struck home.

'You may not want to discuss the matter, but you must see that you really *do* owe me an explanation,' she told him, making a determined effort to keep the burning anger from her voice. There was clearly nothing to be gained by giving vent to her rising fury, and maybe there was still a slight chance that she could persuade him to change his mind. ...?

'I have said all I'm prepared to say on the subject,' he replied coolly. 'I have decided that I do not wish to do business with you — and that is that.'

'But you must give me a reason! It's totally unreasonable not to explain what lies behind your extraordinary decision.'

He shrugged. 'I see no reason to either apologise or explain my decision. And kindly do not use the word "must" when speaking to me. Nobody — *but nobody!* — tells me what I can and cannot do.'

Xavier's sheer arrogance and contempt for other people's feelings was *truly awesome*! Practically unable to believe the evidence of her own ears, Louisa stared at him in amazed bewilderment.

'I don't know what sort of world you think you live in — but it certainly doesn't seem to be the same planet inhabited by the rest of us mortals!' she seethed, too furious now for caution. 'As our business discussions haven't even started, you can hardly be objecting to my way of doing business, right? So the only other reason has to be my sex. In fact, it looks as if your crazy decision is prompted solely by the fact that I'm a woman!'

'You are welcome to come to any conclusion that you wish,' he drawled smoothly, before raising his arm to glance at the watch on his wrist. 'However, I'm not prepared to stand here all day. So I suggest that you do not waste any more of my valuable time with such futile arguments.'

There was no doubt about it: Xavier was absolutely, completely and utterly *unbelievable*!

Louisa couldn't remember a time when she had felt

quite so violently angry with anyone. It wasn't just the blow to her career—severe as that would probably prove to be. But to realise that she'd been somehow cheapened and betrayed by his action was making her feel almost physically sick. How could this man, who clearly could take his pick of any of the world's beautiful women, have played such a despicable cat-and-mouse game with her? Had it been some kind of test? If she had violently repulsed his advances, would he still have allowed her to conduct business with him?

But that didn't make sense, she quickly reminded herself. Xavier had already made his phone call to her London office *before* he'd returned to indulge in a little casual lovemaking. The man was clearly a total *rat*!

'I am still waiting, Louisa, for you to get into the car.' The heavy, ironic sarcasm in the voice interrupting her distraught thoughts seemed to act as a catalyst, pushing her completely over the edge.

'Don't you *dare* to order me around!' she stormed, her overwhelming fury at being treated as a creature of little or no account impelling her to move swiftly towards him. 'Let me tell you, Monsieur d'Erlanger,' she continued through clenched teeth, 'the development which you so admired, at San Raphaël, only got off the ground and was a success due to *my* efforts. It was *I* who bullied the architect and designer into producing their plans on time, and it was *I* who had sole charge of the building operations. So don't try and tell me that I can't deal with a very small, totally insignificant piece of land here in Corsica!' she raged.

'Kindly calm yourself, Louisa!' he retorted curtly. 'Even though you do have hair the colour of carrots, there is no need to scream at me like a fishwife!'

'"*Carrots*". . .?' she cried incredulously, before what was left of her temper spun completely out of control. 'You obviously seem to think that you're God's gift to women—but I think you're pathetic! And if you imagine that I've been behaving like a fishwife, you haven't yet heard the half of what I intend to say to you. . .you miserable apology for a man!'

A second later, Louisa's hand came into sharp

contact with his lean, tanned cheek. But even at the very instant of her action, as the sound of the loud slap seemed to echo and reverberate in the air about them, she felt almost sick with self-disgust.

What on earth could be happening to her? Never, in all her life, had she ever struck anyone in anger or fury. And it was no excuse to tell herself that she'd been provoked beyond reason by his cyncial arrogance.

For a long moment it seemed as though Xavier was every bit as shocked and stunned by her action as she was. Raising his fingers to touch the red mark on his flesh, his dark eyes glittered with a fierce rage that almost scorched her trembling body.

'So — I'm "pathetic", am I? It's time someone taught you a lesson, you impertinent, carrot-headed *vixen*!' he hissed through clenched teeth.

His handsome features were twisted to a fearsome mask of fury as he quickly gripped hold of her wrists, his fingers biting like talons into her soft flesh. She tried to escape, to pull away — but all in vain as she found herself jerked swiftly forward, hard up against his rigidly angry figure. Trembling with fear against his tall frame, the smouldering rage in his eyes seemed to touch off a primitive, mutual antagonism that blazed savagely between them.

'No one — especially not a woman! — strikes a Corsican without reprisal!' he ground out harshly.

Louisa could feel her heart beating frantically. She was feeling sick, and unable to tear her eyes away from the mark of her fingers on his tanned cheek.

'You. . .you asked for it!' she gasped huskily, trying not to give way to the tremors of fear spiralling up and down her backbone.

'And you have most certainly asked for *this*!' Xavier grated, and a moment later his mouth was on hers, angry and contemptuous, as though he intended to completely drain her of the will to defy him ever again.

She felt faint, her heartbeat almost stopping beneath the punishing force of his lips. She couldn't move. His hand still gripped her wrists tightly behind her, while the other swiftly removed the combs from her hair, pulling on the tumbling locks until she was arched vulnerably backwards, her soft lips crushed beneath his hard mouth as he maintained a punishing pressure — the lesson he seemed resolutely determined that she should learn.

Held in a firm, vice-like grip against the taut maleness of his body, she was ashamed to discover that what he intended as a fierce, savage punishment should somehow have ignited a powerful sexual chemistry which crackled like forked lightning between them.

With her soft breasts crushed so tightly against his hard chest, she at last recognised the truth: that the soft black leather jacket, like the expensive suit and accessories which he had been wearing yesterday, were merely the civilised adornments which masked the raw savagery of this man — a true descendant of his vengeful Corsican forefathers.

Helplessly trapped within the steely grip of his embrace, she knew that he was using this kiss as an act of revenge — both for daring to defy him, and to impress his iron will upon her — the hard arrogance of his flesh demanding nothing less than her complete submission.

As her body trembled weakly against him, she could feel his lips softening for a moment before he slowly lifted his head, the flickering gold specks in his dark eyes having an almost hypnotic effect on her shattered emotions.

'Have you learnt your lesson, Louisa? Or do I have to repeat the punishment?' he taunted softly, before giving a short bark of sardonic laughter at her strangled, horrified gasp of fear and intimidation.

CHAPTER FOUR

THE journey back to Ajaccio was a complete nightmare!

'Boiling with rage' was hardly an adequate description of how she felt, Louisa decided as the black Ferrari swiftly left the port of Propriano behind, gathering speed as it swept down the road to Ajaccio, the town of Napoléon's birth.

She still had no idea why Xavier had taken such an extraordinary decision to have her removed—lock, stock and barrel—from the negotiations over the land he owned. It wasn't as though it was likely to be a complicated transaction. In fact, thinking back over her career, she could recall many bargaining sessions with so many complex factors that she'd needed all the skill of Machiavelli to bring matters to a successful conclusion. But, as Louisa felt like shouting at the dreadful man, the whole point was that she *had* achieved the impossible; she *had* managed to arrange deals which had succeeded in satisfying all the interested parties.

But now, here was Xavier—surely the original prototype of the male-chauvinist pig?—insisting that she be removed from the negotiation. And she still didn't know why he had acted in such an arbitrary manner.

How she'd managed to force her trembling body into the passenger seat of the Ferrari, Louisa had no idea. And, although she was by now slowly recovering from Xavier's determined assault on her senses, she still felt a deep, burning sense of injustice at the way she'd been treated.

Neither of them had addressed one word to each other since the beginning of their journey back to Ajaccio. The atmosphere within the close confines of the vehicle was so tense and nerve-racking that she was certain that it could almost be cut with a knife. His

56

long tanned fingers were clenched tightly on the driving-wheel, and, although it might have been her imagination, it seemed that he was driving through the dangerous-looking hairpin bends of the coastal route even faster than he had on the relatively straight road leading out of the port.

'For goodness' sake!' she gasped as they rounded a corner, only missing another car on the road by a hair's breadth. 'There's no need to drive like a maniac! Why don't you slow down?'

'Are you presuming to tell me how to drive this car?' he demanded, the knuckles of the hands gripping the wheel whitening with suppressed fury and tension.

'I don't care what you do,' she retorted grimly. 'My only concern is to arrive back at my hotel in one piece!'

'*Quelle insolence*!' he growled menacingly. 'Kindly remain silent. I have had quite enough of your effrontery for one day!'

'Oh, really?' Louisa enquired with deadly sweetness. In some strange way, she was deriving considerable satisfaction at Xavier's loss of temper. In fact, his clear anger and frustration, as he swore grimly beneath the sound of the car's engine, served only to act as a soothing balm to her troubled spirits.

Although she might have grounds for protesting at the excessive speed of the vehicle, she actually had no real fear that they would crash. As much as she might loathe the rigidly angry figure sitting beside her, there was no doubt that he was a superb driver, handling the powerful vehicle with consummate ease. It was for that very reason that she now had no compunction about deliberately setting out to upset him even further.

Not only had he treated her abominably, but it was definitely about time that Xavier d'Erlanger—alias Comte Cinarchesi!—learned one of the hard, tough rules of life. As an American colleague had once said to her, 'If you can't take the heat—you'd better stay out of the kitchen!'

'I've been thinking,' she mused slowly, careful to keep all expression out of her voice. 'I can't help wondering exactly *why* you should find the fact that

I'm a woman quite so disturbing. After all, you don't *look* like a man who's frightened of the female sex. Still. . .' she gave a careless shrug of her shoulders, before adding airily, '. . .I suppose you never can tell about men, nowadays.'

'*Careful*. . .!' she added with a quick shriek as Xavier turned to glare at her, momentarily losing control of the vehicle, whose wheels suddenly wobbled and spun dangerously across the road for a moment. 'For heaven's sake — kindly keep your eyes on the road!'

'Are you daring to query my *masculinity*?' he demanded incredulously, clearly so overcome by her temerity in having the nerve to raise such a ridiculous question that he completely ignored the grave insult to his driving skill.

'Who, me?' she drawled with well-simulated surprise. 'Really, Xavier — how could I possibly know anything about your sexual inclinations?'

He gave a grim bark of spine-chilling laughter. 'I rather thought that I had given you an adequate demonstration only half an hour ago. However, if you wish me to repeat the punishment, I am quite prepared to do so. It would seem that, like your brother, you also must be taught a lesson which you will not forget in a hurry!'

Louisa gave a gasp as enlightenment finally dawned. '*Of course*! That's what this is all about, isn't it?'

'I have no idea what you're talking about.'

'Oh, yes, you do!' she snapped. 'Not only were you absolutely *furious* at finding yourself having to deal with a woman, but, in arranging my removal from our business negotiations, you are also getting your own back against my stepbrother — for what you consider his bad treatment of your niece.'

Louisa almost choked as she added, 'I simply don't understand how you can be *so* utterly cruel and ruthless. Don't you care about other people at all? Don't you understand that I may well lose my job, simply because of your stupid idea of taking revenge against my brother?'

He was silent for some moments before saying

firmly, 'My reson for dispensing with your services was neither due to your sex, nor to your brother's actions. I have not changed my mind about Monsieur Kendall's disgraceful conduct towards my niece. However, I give you my solemn word of honour that what I say is the truth,' he added strongly and firmly.

Louisa shook her head helplessly. She no longer knew *what* to believe. In fact, ever since she'd arrived on this island yesterday, she'd never felt entirely in charge of her life. Events and personalities—particularly that of Xavier—had all seemed to conspire against her. She felt as if she was being completely swept off her normally sensible feet, and no longer seeming to have any control over her own destiny.

Was Xavier telling the truth? He had sounded genuinely sincere in his denial, just now. But what other possible reason could he have for her dismissal?

If she wasn't feeling so tired and exhausted by the emotional trauma of the day's events, she might be able to think more clearly about the situation. However, aware of the fact that she had yet to tell Xavier about the phone conversation she'd had with Jamie this morning—and taking account of the fact that he appeared to have calmed down somewhat—she gave him an edited version of her stepbrother's confession.

'It seems that I owe you an apology,' she added grudgingly. 'But I can promise you that I really had no idea matters had gone quite so far between your niece and Jamie.'

'I am prepared to accept your apology, and your assurance that you didn't know the true facts of the situation.' Xavier replied with his usual cool arrogance. 'But that does not solve Marie-Thérèse's problem, does it?'

Louisa gave a heavy sigh. 'I can't speak for your niece, of course. However, Jamie assures me that there can be no question of. . .' She hesitated for a moment, her cheeks reddening with embarrassment. 'I mean. . . he says that he's convinced she can't be pregnant.'

'Marie-Thérèse? *Expecting a baby*? The very idea is completely ridiculous!' He gave a snort of derision.

'Well, at least that's *one* area of agreement between you and my stepbrother,' she retorted wryly, relieved to have her dire fears about his niece so swiftly laid to rest. 'In fact, it seems that there never was any reason for you to be unduly worried. I understand that the girl was wise enough to take proper precautions.'

She was astounded by Xavier's reaction to her words.

'Are you suggesting that my niece was not a virgin?' he demanded furiously.

'Oh, for heaven's sake!' Louisa gave a weak laugh. 'I'm not saying that I approve of what's happened. However, you really must face the fact that many young girls nowadays have had some sort of sexual experience. And, in any case, you seem to be deliberately misunderstanding me, because I was just saying how sensible I thought your niece had been.'

Once again, it seemed as though she had said entirely the wrong thing. Unfortunately, it wasn't immediately clear from the tirade of fast, heavily idiomatic French exactly what Xavier was objecting to. What *was* clear, however, was the constant reiteration that his niece had been 'ruined' by Jamie, and that he had every intention of making sure, in the very near future, that both Lord Armstrong and his daughter were made aware of the fact.

'That's not fair!'

'I am not interested in being fair,' he ground out furiously through clenched teeth. 'My Corsican ancestors believed in claiming an eye for an eye, and a tooth for a tooth. Think yourself lucky, *mademoiselle*,' he added menacingly, 'that you are living in the twentieth century. Not so long ago, there would have been no reason why I should not take vengeance on your family by ruining *your* reputation—just as my niece's has been ruined. Although even then I do not believe I could have brought myself to soil my hands—not with a woman such as you!'

Almost convinced that she had strayed into the middle of a Victorian melodrama, or some Gothic horror novel, Louisa quickly decided that there was no point in responding to any more of this man's dire, menacing threats.

For one thing, there didn't seem to be any way in which she could get Xavier to see sense about the relationship between Jamie and his niece. Admittedly, she had her own old-fashioned views about love and fidelity, but that didn't mean she couldn't take a sensible view on general sexual matters. Surely it was better to make sure that an unwanted child wasn't brought into the world than to put one's head in the sand and ignore the whole problem?

However, Xavier clearly had a closed mind on the subject. And for them to be continually trading insults with each other seemed entirely pointless. Especially as, she miserably acknowledged to herself, she seemed unable either to win any of the arguments, or to puncture his amazing arrogance.

Looking out of the windscreen, she noticed that they were approaching the outskirts of Ajaccio, and therefore she would only be forced to remain within this vehicle for a few more minutes. So it seemed that a dignified silence would appear to be her best and indeed her only option.

By the time he drew the fast sports car up outside her hotel, Louisa had just about reached the end of her tether. Swiftly releasing her seatbelt and opening the passenger door, she leaped out of the car. Pausing only to savagely inform Xavier that she never *ever* wanted to see him again, she dashed quickly up the steps, intent on reaching the sanctuary of her room as fast as possible.

Why had absolutely *nothing* gone right since her arrival here in Corsica? Louisa asked herself in despair as she banged loudly on the ancient, massive oak door of Xavier's mountain-top castle.

Drenched to the skin, and shivering with fright, as the thunder and lightning crashed terrifyingly overhead, it was definitely no help to know that she had only herself to blame for her present predicament.

She had been so intent on escaping from Xavier

yesterday afternoon that she'd had no thought of
anything other than of putting as much distance
between herself and the dreadful man as possible.
After rushing into her hotel room, she'd thrown herself
down on to the bed, staring blindly up at the ceiling as
she tried to think what she was going to do about her
job. It had been too late in the day to ring her office in
London. And in any case, it would be far better for
her—and her future employment prospects—to try to
reach Neville Frost at home, later that night.

Unfortunately, until then, there had been nothing
she could do. Despite running the disastrous events of
the day back and forth through her tired mind, she still
hadn't been able to find any clues to Xavier's extraordinary behaviour. All she'd succeeded in doing, in
fact, had been to give herself a thumping headache.

Wearily going through to her *en-suite* bathroom to
find some aspirins, Louisa had decided that maybe a
shower, and a change of clothes, might succeed in
making her feel slightly better. And it was true that by
the time she had returned to her bedroom she had
been feeling a good deal more refreshed, even if there
had seemed little she could do to banish her deep sense
of failure and depression. It was in this heavy, miserable state of mind that she'd first discovered her
handbag was missing, although it was several moments
before she could bring herself to face the hideous
truth—that she must have left it in Xavier's car!

Still clutching a thick towel about her damp body,
Louisa had slumped helplessly down on to a chair in
front of her dressing-table, practically weeping with
frustration. Because, far from being just an unfortunate, careless accident, the loss of her handbag was
likely to prove a *complete* disaster.

Containing not only her money, her credit cards and
international driving licence, the handbag also held her
small business Filofax. Between its red leather covers
lay all the names and addresses of her clients, her diary
appointments for the rest of the year, and—something
which Xavier would be sure to find *very* interesting—

all the details, figures and estimates she'd made regarding the development of his land.

But that wasn't all! By far the most awful, *disastrous* consequence of her carelessness was that she now had no alternative: she was going to have to contact Xavier once again.

Catching a brief glimpse of her apprehensive green eyes and the pale, chalky pallor of her cheeks in the dressing-table mirror, Louisa had taken a deep breath and tried to calm down. But there had seemed little she could do to control her rising panic. Just the thought of having anything more to do with the awful man was enough to bring her out in a cold sweat.

Even now, almost twenty-four hours later, as she beat frantically on the old oak-panelled door of Xavier's castle—cursing him hard and long for choosing to live in such a remote, mountainous part of the island—Louisa wasn't just freezing cold and soaked to the skin, she was also feeling quite sick with nerves.

Following the discovery of her missing handbag yesterday, the hotel staff had been very helpful. When it appeared that Comte Cinarchesi's large office block was closed for the weekend, they had given her the address of his mountain-top castle, near the town of Corte. Situated in the centre of the island, some seventy kilometres away from Ajaccio, the ancient edifice had been totally renovated from the derelict, ruinous state in which Comte Cinarchesi had apparently inherited it from an uncle, some years ago. Unfortunately, while the hotel manager had assured her that the castle was the last word in luxury, and fairly bristling with modern technical aids, it seemed that the Comte valued his privacy. Because, try as she might, Louisa had been unable to discover a telephone number for the castle.

Trust Xavier to be ex-directory! she'd thought grimly, realising that she now had no alternative but to go to his home in the mountains. Only how on earth was she going to get there?

It had proved difficult to hire a car without her international driving licence. Luckily, the hotel man-

ager had been very helpful, arranging for her to borrow
a vehicle which belonged to a member of his family. 'It
isn't a brand new car, of course,' the manager had
shrugged. 'But my cousin assures me that you will have
no trouble in reaching your destination.'

When she'd first set eyes on the ancient Renault
earlier this morning, Louisa had been forced to quickly
remind herself that beggars couldn't be choosers.
Unfortunately, her severe doubts about the car, which
looked as though it was about to give up the ghost any
minute, had soon proved to be realised. Not only had
the engine sounded as if it had a terminal case of acute
bronchitis, but the coughing and spluttering issuing
from beneath the bonnet, as she'd driven slowly up the
steep and winding roads of the mountains, had been
truly frightening. Her nervous state hadn't been helped
by the way the bright morning sunshine had soon
disappeared behind heavy grey clouds, which had
grown increasingly darker and more threatening with
every passing mile.

Ever since childhood, Louisa had been scared to
death of thunder and lightning. And, just as she
glimpsed her first sight of Xavier's huge stone castle,
perched high up on a mountain crag, the storm had
broken loudly over her head. Deafened by loudly
crashing rolls of thunder, quickly followed by mind-
dazzling flashes of sheet-lightning, Louisa had found
herself in the midst of a terrifying thunderstorm.

Almost petrified with fear, she'd struggled to keep
up the momentum of the car, against a flood of water
pouring down the road off the mountains high above.
And then, just as she'd turned a corner and could see
the entrance to the castle, the old Renault had given
one last final, desperate cough, before coming to a
shuddering and silent halt.

Trying in vain to restart the car, and realising that it
was only a few hundred yards to the massive front door
of the castle, Louisa had taken a deep breath and
dashed through the storm. But, by the time she'd
managed to reach the door — gasping and completely
out of breath, as well as totally soaked to the skin — it

now seemed the final straw not to be able to make anyone hear the sound of her frantic knocking. Nor was there any response to her repeated distraught yanking of the heavy old iron doorbell.

'Help! *Help*. . .!' she was yelling hoarsely, tears of frustration and despair joining the heavy rain beating down on her face, when she heard a sudden clang as heavy bolts on the other side of the door were withdrawn, and it swung slowly open.

A tall figure stood framed in the doorway, and for a brief second she thought it was Xavier. But as she swept the thick coils of sopping wet hair from her eyes, Louisa saw that she was facing a tall, elderly man in a dark suit.

Shivering so much that she could hardly speak, she tried to explain why she'd come to the castle. But she wasn't at all sure he understood what she was saying, since he merely gestured for her to follow him before turning and walking swiftly away.

Squelching after the man, her shoes so sodden with water that they would clearly never be the same again, she eventually found herself being led into a huge, cavernous dark hall. It was so large that the high roof was completely lost to sight in the dim lighting, which threw ghostly shadows on to the thick stone walls. Gesturing her shivering figure over to the massive marble fireplace, which seemed to be burning practically half a tree, the man disappeared from view.

It seemed to Louisa as though she'd been shivering and trembling beside the fire for hours. Then she caught the sound of footsteps, swiftly followed by a sharp 'click', and the whole of the vast space was suddenly flooded with light.

'*Mon Dieu*!' a familiar hard voice exclaimed from the far end of the hall. 'What are *you* doing here?'

After the shadowy darkness, it took Louisa some moments to adjust her eyes to the sudden, brilliant light shed by the row of large brass chandeliers hanging down the length of the huge hall.

Despite being cold, wet and miserable, she could only stare up in awe at the vast space, which she realised must be the original great hall of the castle. Now, with hundreds of lamps blazing, Louisa could see that the rough-hewn stone walls were covered with ancient weapons, and large old family portraits in heavily ornate gold frames. The stark severity of this enormous space was enlivened by the sparkling, jewel-like colours of ancient family banners, hanging suspended from brass rods high up on the great stone walls, which rose in stern and sombre magnificence to the vaulted ceiling way above her head.

While she had been absorbing her surroundings, Xavier had been striding down the long hall towards her, the hard sound of his heels on the ancient stone floors sounding like the approach of doom as they echoed around the huge space.

'Louisa! What *have* you been doing?' he demanded, his dark brows drawn together in a deep frown as he viewed her drenched, soaking wet figure.

'What does it l-look as if I've been d-doing?' she retorted, shivering so hard that she found it difficult to enunciate her words properly. 'I got caught in the storm, and I think I'm about to die of c-cold—or possibly pneumonia!' she added weakly, her body shaking uncontrollably as she quickly turned back to the fire, holding her trembling hands out towards the blazing logs.

His shocked expression at the sight of her bedraggled figure had said it all, she thought miserably. And it was no consolation to know that forces beyond her control had resulted in her looking such a perfect fright. With the warmth of the fire now causing her soaking clothes to give off clouds of damp steam, and with her hair in long, tangled rat's-tails, dripping wetly down into the puddle of water already spreading about her feet, Louisa knew that she must look a truly awful sight.

'But what has happened? Have you been in an accident?'

'No—the car just died on me,' she mumbled helplessly. 'I suppose it's my own f-fault. . . I got lost, once or twice, and——'

'Come—you need to have a hot bath and a change

of clothes,' Xavier said firmly, moving over to the side
of the fireplace to tug at a thick rope, before returning
to take hold of her arm.

'No, I. . .I can't st-stay here,' she stuttered, trying to
stop her teeth from chattering. 'I just want to get hold
of my handbag and——'

'Yes, yes—all in good time,' he said impatiently.
'Come, Louisa,' he said, his fingers tightening on her
arm in a grip that brooked no denial.

She stared up at the man towering over her, her
dazed mind refusing to function normally as he firmly
propelled her shivering figure away from the fire,
leading her back across the hall.

The next few minutes seemed to pass in a haze, not
helped by the fact that, with her wringing wet hair still
falling in damp coils about her face, Louisa could
hardly see where she was going. He seemed to be
forcibly steering her down a long, stone-walled corridor, where they were met by a plump middle-aged
woman.

'Ah, there you are, Rosa,' he said, quickly cutting
across the woman's exclamations of shock and surprise
at the sight of Louisa's drenched figure, swiftly ordering
a hot meal to be prepared for his unexpected guest.

In a daze, as if her dash through the storm towards
the castle had taken all her reserves of physical and
mental strength, Louisa found herself moving like an
automaton, allowing Xavier to lead her up a wide oak
staircase, along a corridor and through a glamorous
suite of rooms towards a large marble bathroom.

As she gazed around the vast, luxuriously appointed
room, she suddenly remembered the hotel manager's
enthusiastic words, back in Ajaccio. 'Comte Cinarchesi's
ancient castle is truly magnificent!' he'd told her, before
lowering his voice and adding confidentially, 'They say
that he has spent *millions* on its refurbishment. His
uncle, the old Comte, had allowed the castle to fall
into disrepair, for many years.' The manager had
tapped his head with a finger. 'The poor old man was
very eccentric. Quite mad, in fact!'

'You need a hot bath.' Xavier's harsh voice broke into her thoughts.

'I can't possibly. . . I must have made a terrible mess,' she muttered helplessly, trying to look back over her shoulder at what she was sure must be a trail of wet, muddy footprints over the thick velvety pile of pale gold carpeting.

'It is nothing,' he said dismissively, leaving her side to turn on the taps of quite the most enormous bath she had ever seen. Liberally pouring a stream of fragrant bath oil into the water, he abruptly told Louisa to remove her wet clothing—'*immédiatement!*'

'What. . .?'

Xavier looked at the girl, whose sodden figure was swaying with fatigue and weariness. 'It is important that you get into a hot bath straight away,' he told her slowly and firmly, as if talking to a small child.

But it seemed to take an age before his words slowly began to penetrate her dazed mind. And, as she stood there, gazing at the hot, pine-scented water with a desperate longing, he gave an impatient click of his tongue and quickly strode across the room towards her. Before she knew what was happening, he began to undo the small buttons on her dress.

'No! I. . .I'm quite capable of undressing myself,' she protested breathlessly, moving hurriedly away from him, only to find her spine coming hard up against the cold marble wall of the bathroom.

'There's no need to act like a frightened virgin!' he told her drily. 'It is important that you get into a hot bath, and as soon as possible. So, either you take off your wet dress—or I intend to do it for you!'

His words had the effect of jerking her out of her state of dazed confusion, and she quickly assured him that she was perfectly capable of removing her own clothes. But in her haste to prove her point, Louisa found herself fumbling clumsily with the fiddly small pearl buttons running down the front of her soaking wet green cotton dress. A moment later her hands were quickly brushed aside as long, tanned fingers deftly and swiftly performed the job for her.

'Xavier—please!'

'This is no time to be prudish,' he told her with blunt impatience. Suiting his actions to his words, he quickly seized the damp folds of what had once been a pretty dress, ruthlessly ignoring her muffled protests as he swept it up over her head. Swearing under his breath at the wet material, which clung so stubbornly to her damp shoulder-blades, Xavier quickly threw aside the garment, before crouching down on his heels to remove her sodden, waterlogged shoes.

'This must be the first and last time that Xavier's ever knelt at a woman's feet!' she told herself, a hysterical bubble of laughter rising in her throat. Only to be thrown into immediate confusion as she realised, from his grunt of wry laughter, that she had unwittingly voiced her thoughts aloud.

'Not *entirely* right, my dear Louisa. But I must admit that it has been a long time since I did so!' he agreed with sardonic amusement as he rose again to his full height.

Clasping her slim arms about her shivering figure, now only clothed in a frilly lace bra and pants, Louisa could only wildly ask herself why she'd been so certain that she was cold. With Xavier's dark, gleaming eyes sweeping over her almost nude body, a deep heat seemed to be flooding through every fibre of her being.

'There's no need. . . I mean, I'm perfectly able to do the rest by myself,' she muttered nervously.

'Yes, I'm sure you are,' he purred softly as he turned to leave the room. 'But I give you fair warning, Louisa. You have precisely *one minute* in which to do so. Otherwise, I shall most certainly strip those fragile pieces of lace from your body—and throw you into the bath myself!'

CHAPTER FIVE

FLOATING in the warm, scented water, Louisa almost groaned out loud with relief and pleasure as she felt life returning to her frozen limbs. It was some minutes before the mist began clearing from her equally frozen mind, and she began to realise that she hadn't been at all polite to Xavier. In fact, to put it bluntly, she must have appeared extremely rude when, true to his word, he'd returned to the bathroom.

Completely ignoring her shocked cry of 'Get out of here!'—slightly muffled as she hurriedly sank down beneath the foaming bubbles—Xavier had merely lifted one dark, aristocratic eyebrow.

'My dear Louisa—there is no need to become so excited!' he'd drawled with amusement. 'I have actually seen a naked female body before, you know.'

'Not *this* body, you haven't!' she'd snapped, her cheeks blushing a fiery red with embarrassment.

'Very true,' he had murmured sardonically. 'However, I can assure you that I look forward to our becoming better—how shall I put it?—better acquainted with each other, very shortly.'

'Go away, you foul man. *G-get lost!*'

Maddeningly, he had merely greeted her spluttered words of baffled fury with a caustic, cynical laugh, before turning to leave the room.

Xavier was obviously totally impossible! So why on earth was she now feeling slightly ashamed, and guiltily aware that she hadn't been at all polite to the foul man?

Surely it was crazy to be worried about displaying bad manners? Especially when there was no doubt that Xavier's amazingly arrogance was enough to try the patience of a saint! But taking into account their extremely violent quarrel yesterday—and also the fact that she'd suddenly arrived here, at his castle, completely out of the blue—Louisa had to admit that he'd been very kind and considerate. Those weren't the usual adjectives she might use when thinking about him, of course. However, she really couldn't find an excuse for not having thanked him for allowing her to use his bathroom. And there seemed no doubt that it *was* his own, private bathroom. Not only were there many large crystal bottles of hideously expensive after-shave and cologne standing on glass shelves beside the twin marble basins, but it looked as if it must be his dressing-gown which she could see hanging on the back of the door.

Unfortunately, it wasn't just her manners which had completely deserted her, Louisa told herself dismally. It looked as if she'd been going completely to pieces ever since her arrival in Corsica. What she liked to think of as her normally keen, sharp intelligence seemed to have become dangerously befuddled. Even the simple ability to think in a straight line had some-how seemed almost beyond her during these last few difficult days. Her troubled, disturbed nights had prob-ably contributed to the ever growing sense of disorien-tation and mounting confusion. However, she could now see that she'd been very unfair in placing the blame for the rapid decline in her mental and physical condition on this beautiful island.

Lying here in this opulent bathroom relishing the palatial luxury of the heavy gold taps and the ornately carved mirrors on every wall, while soaking in the depths of a vast bath, she finally realised *just* how wrong she'd been. And with the caressing warmth and comfort of the oily, pine-scented water gently soothing her tired body, Louisa at last understood that it wasn't Corsica which lay at the root of her problems—*it was Xavier*!

It was a really awful conclusion to come to, but it was the only one that made any kind of sense. It certainly would account for her feverish, nervous reac-tion whenever she found herself in close proximity to his tall, dynamic figure. It would also explain why she seemed unable to resist being drawn to him, like a fluttering moth to the flame.

Although Louisa could hardly bear to face the fact, it seemed as if she had no choice but to accept the logical and devastating truth: that she—poor fool!—appeared to be totally infatuated with that really awful man, Xavier d'Erlanger, Comte Cinarchesi!

How *could* such a disastrous, mad passion have suddenly hit her out of the blue like this? Was it *really* possible to fall hook, line and sinker for a man in just two short days? The whole idea seemed totally incredible!

Sinking even lower in the bath-water, Louisa couldn't help giving a deep, heartfelt groan of despair. Although she'd never been attracted to anyone in this way before, she knew there was no chance that these strong, powerful emotions could lead anywhere but to deep unhappiness. Unfortunately, while she might have had very little experience of these matters in the past, it was clearly obvious that she'd fallen for *absolutely* the wrong man! With Xavier's contemptuous arrogance of those he considered beneath him, and a haughty, imperious attitude to life which was almost beyond belief, she wasn't even sure that she liked him, for heaven's sake!

Quite apart from anything else—and, just to make matters ten times worse—there was the lowering thought that she couldn't possibly be the only one to feel such an insane, fatal attraction to the man. In fact she was quite certain that there must be hundreds of women who were likely to be ensnared by his strikingly handsome features and obvious wealth. Not to mention the others—like herself, alas!—who found themselves helplessly enticed and bewitched by the dark, magical enchantment of his overwhelming sensual appeal.

She'd simply *got* to pull herself together! Louisa told herself roughly. Sitting up in the bath, and briskly sponging her face with cold water, she desperately tried to cast aside her feelings of gloom and misery.

It had all seemed to happen with the speed of light! In fact it was difficult for her to realise that it had only been two days since she'd first met Xavier, and found herself enmeshed in such a hopeless state of infatuation. So surely it shouldn't take much longer to force herself out of it? But at the thought of just how quickly she'd fallen victim to Xavier's magnetic attraction, she realised that her caustic, scathing treatment of Jamie had been very unjust. In the light of her present problems, his brief affair with Marie-Thérèse now seemed entirely understandable, and she was ashamed how dismissive and contemptuous of his weakness she had been.

In fact the only small crumb of comfort she could find in this whole miserable affair was in remembering her stepbrother's remark that it took 'two to tango'. She might be a complete novice in affairs of the heart, but even she could see that such a one-sided force of emotion—however strong—must eventually wither and die from lack of nourishment. And since there was absolutely *no* chance of Xavier's experiencing the same feelings about her, she must do her very best to ruthlessly crush her totally foolish, hopeless infatuation for the man.

A loud banging on the door brought an abrupt end to her dismal, introspective thoughts.

'Are you all right in there?' Xavier's disembodied voice demanded.

'Yes—yes, I'm fine,' she called back quickly, anxious not to give him any reason to invade the bathroom again. 'I'll be out in a minute—just as soon as I've washed my hair,' she added, trying hard to sound bright and confident.

When she was finally ready to leave the bathroom she discovered that Xavier must have removed her wet clothing. The only thing she could find to cover her nakedness was a royal blue towelling robe hanging on the back of the door. However, as soon as she slipped it on, she immediately knew that it must belong to Xavier; its material was subtly impregnated with the disturbing, musky scent of his cologne.

Suddenly feeling quite overcome, she leaned weakly against the wall for a moment. And then, catching sight of her flushed cheeks in a nearby mirror, she grimaced at herself with irritation and self-disgust.

She *must* stop being so pathetic! It was only his dressing-gown, for heaven's sake! Even if she was temporarily caught up in the toils of helpless lust and infatuation, there was surely no need for her to over-react to the situation in such a feeble-minded way?

After giving herself a stern lecture and splashing her face with cold water, Louisa cautiously opened the bathroom door. Barely able to remember the layout of the rooms through which Xavier had originally led her, she hesitantly made her way into what appeared to be a large dressing-room. Her bare feet moving silently over the thickly piled carpet, she passed beneath a high stone arch which led into yet another, softly lit room.

Overcome for a moment by the sheer size and lofty, magnificent grandeur of the bedroom in which she now found herself, Louisa stood staring in amazement at quite the largest four-poster bed she had ever seen. Its tall wooden posts supported an intricate iron frame-work, rising upwards in a gracefully curved tent-shape, which was topped by flamboyant plumes of ostrich feathers. The gold and crimson feathers added a sump-tuous, if somewhat eccentric luxury to the richly embroidered gold and crimson silk hangings draped in long heavy swaths about the bed.

'Ah, there you are — at last!'

At the unexpected sound of Xavier's voice, she almost jumped out of her skin with shock. Quickly spinning around, she saw him put down a book on a small side-table, before rising from the large comfort-able chair in which he'd been sitting.

'I'm sorry. . . I didn't see you over there. I was. . . well, I was just admiring this really quite astonishing bed,' she told him, before suddenly realising that he might get *entirely* the wrong idea from her innocent remark. Feeling a total idiot, she dearly wished that she'd kept her mouth firmly shut.

'Ah, yes. This *lit à la Polonaise* was one of my great-uncle's more engaging follies,' he drawled blandly as he came to stand beside her, raising a quizzical dark eyebrow at the slight flush staining the girl's pale cheeks. 'When I was renovating the castle, my aunt Sophie begged me not to throw it away, and I must admit that I've now become quite fond of it. Besides which——' he gave her a warm, engaging grin, which almost made her heart turn over, '—I have discovered that it is easily the most comfortable bed that I possess.'

'Yes, well—er—it's certainly different!' she muttered breathlessly, turning back to stare blindly at the richly embroidered hangings.

Oh, *help*! What on earth had happened to all the down-to-earth, level-headed advice she'd just been giving herself in the bathroom? Louisa asked herself wildly. Unfortunately, it had taken only one clear sight of this man's lithe and supple grace as he'd strode lazily across the carpet towards her for all sense and logic to immediately vanish from her brain.

It seemed as though an iron band of fear and trepidation was tightening about her chest, making it difficult for her to breathe. And as she tried to control her rapid heartbeat, Louisa did her best to ignore the sensual aura projected by the man standing so close to her. It wasn't an easy task!

In fact she was finding it almost impossible to tear her eyes away from the dark blue-black sheen of his hair, glinting in the soft overhead light of a glass chandelier, as it tumbled loosely down over his well-shaped head, to curl up over the edge of his collar. Neither could she seem to shut her eyes to the cut of his slim dark trousers, topped by a soft silver-grey cashmere sweater over a black shirt, its open neck displaying the strong tanned column of his throat. It was as if everything he wore seemed deliberately designed to emphasise the long, lean body beneath the clothes—the broad shoulders, deep chest and slim waist of a magnificently fit man.

Swallowing hard, Louisa made a determined effort to pull herself together.

'You—um—you mentioned your aunt. Is she staying here with you?'

'Yes—and no,' he replied. 'Aunt Sophie, as she is called, lives here and looks after this castle for me while I'm away in Paris—which is for most of the year.'

His dark gaze swept over the girl's freshly shampooed, red-gold hair falling in a shining stream about her slim shoulers, and her long, shapely legs revealed by the short robe, whose belt was tightly clasped about her thin waist.

'However, I have been remiss in not asking if you enjoyed your bath,' he queried. 'You are certainly looking a good deal better than when I saw you last.'

'I'm fine, and the bath was wonderful! In fact, I really am very grateful to you for rescuing me,' she said, edging nervously away from his tall figure. 'However, I think I ought to be getting back to Ajaccio as soon as possible.'

'But what about your wet clothes? I fear that Rosa will have hardly had time to wash and dry them as yet. And there is, of course, the added problem of your shoes.' He shrugged. 'Alas, they were completely ruined, and I had no choice but to throw them away.'

While Xavier had been speaking, she'd quickly tried to think of how to deal with a 'worst-case scenario'.

'I realise that my clothes might not be dry yet. However, if I could possibly borrow a pair of your trousers—and maybe a shirt and sweater. . .? I could easily return them, just as soon as I got back to Ajaccio. As for the problem of shoes, I'm sure——'

'What are you planning to use for transport? Surely I understood you to say that your car had broken down?' He turned to lean casually against one of the bedposts, regarding her with an air of detached amusement, which she found acutely disturbing.

'Oh, come on!' she snapped nervously. 'We both know that you can easily afford to arrange some transport for me.'

'Well, I'm sorry to disappoint you, my dear Louisa, but what I can or cannot afford is immaterial at the moment,' he drawled blandly. 'I have to tell you that, for the next few hours, you aren't going anywhere,' he announced blandly.

She closed her eyes for a moment and took a deep breath. He was obviously being deliberately aggravating, and it would be foolish of her to rise to the bait. However exasperating this awful man might be — and he most *certainly* was! — she must do her best to keep her temper, whatever the provocation.

'While I *am* grateful for all you've done for me, I really must insist on leaving — right now!' she told him firmly, gritting her teeth when he began to shake his head slowly.

'I find it surprising that you should have so easily forgotten the storm!' he drawled silkily.

'Of course I haven't forgotten it,' she retorted quickly. 'But, since I haven't heard any thunder while I've been here, it's obvious that the storm must have been over some time ago.'

'Not a Corsican thunderstorm — which is every bit as fierce and dramatic as our landscape!' His lips twisted into a grim smile as he took hold of her arm, leading her reluctant figure towards the floor-to-ceiling curtains at the far end of the room.

'The reason you have heard nothing is because the walls of this castle are at least a metre thick,' he continued as he pushed a switch, the heavily padded curtains drawing back on a motorised rail to reveal an enormous plate-glass window practically filling the whole of the wall.

'I can't see any sign of a storm,' Louisa muttered disparagingly, gazing out at a broad expanse of dark, empty sky, with only the shadowy grey shapes of mountains to be seen in the distance.

'My late wife was driving down the mountain during a storm such as this,' he said grimly. 'Unfortunately, Georgette would not listen to my advice. She lost control of her car, and plunged down off the road into a deep ravine.'

'I'm sorry. . . I didn't realise. . .' Louisa muttered, shaken by the harsh note of dark bitterness in his voice as he stared blindly out of the window.

Hesitantly, Louisa tried to explain that she was a careful driver. But, just as she was assuring him that there was no need to worry on her account, her eyes were almost blinded by a brilliant flash of light, whose dazzling magnesium-white flare filled the sky. It was quickly followed by a terrifying and deafening crash of thunder overhead, clearly audible through the large glass window.

'It is only the wildfire of sheet lightning,' Xavier explained as she cried out in fear, throwing herself into his arms and burying her face in the soft folds of his sweater. 'There is no need to be frightened.'

'I can't help it—I've always been absolutely *petrified* of thunder and lightning!' she cried, desperately clutching at the safety of his strong, broad shoulders.

'Believe me—you are really quite safe,' he murmured, gazing down with sardonic amusement at the girl who, only a few moments before, had been clearly trying to evade his grip on her arm. 'There is really no need for you to be afraid,' he added with a low, husky laugh as she clung on to him for dear life.

'I know there isn't!' she muttered, raising her head from the curve of his shoulder, before giving another cry of sheer terror as the lightning seemed to flash right through the glass towards her.

'You need have no fear. This window is made from specially strengthened glass,' he told her reassuringly as he reached out to close the curtains, before his arms closed comfortingly about her frightened, quivering figure.

'I'm sorry to be so. . .so silly,' she muttered helplessly. 'I. . . I'll be all right in a minute. It's just. . . well, some people are terrified of mice or spiders—but with me, it's thunder and lightning.'

'Shush—calm down. There's no need to worry,' he murmured, raising a hand to softly stroke her hair.

Louisa made a determined effort to try to pull herself together. Now that the curtains had been closed again, and with no horrifying flashes of sheet lightning to strike terror into her heart, there seemed no sensible reason for her to be feeling quite so shaken, no cause for her legs to feel as if they would give way beneath her any minute. But she seemed unable to resist the hand which was now gently massaging the tense muscles at the nape of her neck. Neither could she seem to find the strength to protest when his fingers moved to take hold of her chin, tilting it up towards him, so that she was forced to meet his dark eyes.

Drowning in their dark navy blue depths, she couldn't stop herself quivering as a strong force of heat began coursing through her veins, helplessly succumbing to the thrill of rising excitement as his arms gradually tightened about her slim figure, moulding her trembling body closer to his own hard form.

What on earth was happening to her? Nothing in any of her female friends' idle gossip, or anything she'd read in books of romantic fiction, had prepared her for the shock waves of sensuality and sick longing which now seemed to be filling every fibre of her being. Maybe it was the unnatural freedom of her naked form beneath Xavier's robe, but she suddenly felt a completely insane, feverish desire to feel the cool touch of his hands caressing her naked body, a desperate craving for the hard pressure of his lips on hers.

It was so still and quiet. And yet she could almost feel damp beads of perspiration forming on her brow as she strugled to control a painful, deep pulsating ache in the depths of her stomach.

Then suddenly—without warning—his features tightened into a bleak, harsh expression. She heard him give a muffled curse beneath his breath, as she found herself abruptly set free of his embrace. Trembling, she stared helplessly up at him, her mind totally blank of any rational thought or action.

'I think a glass of brandy might make you feel better, hmm?'

As the abrasive, rasping note in his hard voice echoed around the large room, Louisa could only give a slight nod. Her mouth felt suddenly dry with rising tension as he led her back across the room, before slowly lowering her down into a comfortable chair. Thankfully sinking into its cushioned depths, she leaned back, closing her eyes for a moment as she fought to control her trembling limbs.

The violent flashes of lightning had completely taken her by surprise, but she knew that it had been total *madness* for her to have sought shelter within Xavier's arms. Even now, she could still feel the strength of his hard, firm body against hers, still savour the musky, aromatic scent of his cologne and the warm comfort of his soft sweater against her cheek.

It seemed an almost herculean task to force her shattered mind and body into some sort of cohesive action. But she knew that she must try; she *must* make an immediate, determined effort to leave this castle — as quickly as possible!

'Louisa. . .?'

Deeply immersed in a heavy cloud of gloom and despondency, Louisa opened her startled eyes to find Xavier staring down at her with a stern expression on his face.

'Drink this,' he commanded roughly as he handed her a glass. 'You will feel better when you've had some cognac.'

'Thank you. I — er — I'm really feeling quite all right now,' she breathed huskily. Forcing herself to sit up straight and trying to control her trembling hands, she buried her nose in the glass of amber liquid.

'You will also feel much better when you've had some food,' he said firmly. 'I suggest that we go downstairs where my housekeeper, Rosa, will by now have prepared a small meal for you. But first,' he added over his shoulder as he walked swiftly away towards his dressing-room, 'I must find something for you to wear on your feet.'

'There's really no need for you to bother,' she muttered quickly.

'There is every need — especially since I have no wish for you to catch a cold,' he said curtly on his return to the room.

Louisa dubiously eyed the large pair of casual loafers in his hands. 'I really don't think —'

'I am very fond of this castle. But, with its thick stone walls, it can be chilly and damp at times. So, although these are not exactly what you might call *"chic"*. . .!' he grinned, suddenly seeming to throw off his abrasive mood as he handed her the shoes '. . .they should help to keep you warm.'

He was such a surprising man, Louisa thought confusedly as she eased her feet into the shoes, which were, of course, far too large for her. One moment Xavier would be acting like a bear with a sore head, and then — almost in the twinkling of an eye — he could suddenly become amazingly kind and considerate.

'I am very grateful for your help and. . .and I'm sorry to be such a nuisance,' she muttered as she rose to her feet. Taking a cautious step forward, she was surprised to hear him give a short bark of sardonic laughter.

'My dear Louisa — you look almost as amazing as that ridiculous bed of mine! With those "canal boats" on your feet, and dressed in that short towelling robe, no one would ever guess that you were a sophisticated career woman. In fact. . .' he grinned '. . .you look more like a sixteen-year-old schoolgirl!'

Charming! she thought grimly, wondering why on earth she should be attracted to such a thoroughly disagreeable man. But she was far too preoccupied with carefully sliding her feet in the enormous loafers over the slippery velvet pile of the carpet to be able to think of a suitably crushing reply.

However, by the time she was clumping down the stairs in the wake of his tall figure, she'd managed to regain her sense of proportion. The awful man was probably right about her appearance, she realised, and she was just giving herself a stern lecture on the evils of false pride and vanity when Xavier led her into what he described as his private sitting-room.

After the austere grandeur of the great hall downstairs, and the sheer opulent luxury of his bedroom suite, this 'sitting-room' came as a complete surprise. It was, quite simply, one of the most charming, warm and welcoming rooms she'd ever seen.

Of course it was large — vast, in fact — but the leather covers of the books lining the stone walls gave off a comforting glow, as did the deep colours of the Persian silk rugs spread over the dark crimson carpet covering the floor.

Gazing at the large stone fireplace, with its blazing logs throwing a flickering light on to the wide, comfortable sofas, deep armchairs and the large, ancient pieces of clearly priceless furniture, Louisa almost sighed out loud with envy. Xavier might have lavished a huge amount of money on doing up this castle, but she could only feel that it had definitely been worth every franc!

'Why don't you sit down by the fire, and make yourself comfortable, hmm?' he suggested, leading her over to where a tray had been placed on a small table, in front of a wide sofa. 'And please do try and consume the soup while it is hot. Otherwise, I fear Rosa will be very cross with me for not looking after you properly,' he added, shaking his dark head in mock-sorrow.

Unfortunately, despite the appetising meal set out before her, Louisa was dismayed to discover that she couldn't seem to do justice to either the delicious *bouillabaisse*, made from locally caught fish, or the beautifully presented *salade Roscovite*.

However, her anger on discovering that her missing handbag was no longer in Xavier's possession might well have contributed to her lack of appetite.

CHAPTER SIX

'YOU did *what*?'

Louisa stared at Xavier with dazed eyes, hardly able to believe what he was saying. Surely he must be joking? He couldn't *really* be saying that, after all her efforts, her ghastly journey to this castle had been completely unnecessary?

'But, my dear Louisa—I was merely trying to be helpful,' he drawled smoothly. 'I sent my chauffeur down to Ajaccio with your purse early this morning. Of course, I don't know what time you left your hotel.' He shrugged. 'However, I gave my driver, Franco, very clear instructions. In fact, I imagine that the manager has already placed it carefully in his hotel safe.'

'I just *don't* believe it!' she groaned, glowering across the room at the handsome man lounging so elegantly back in his chair.

To be told that she'd struggled through the frightening storm, and been totally soaked to the skin for absolutely *no* reason was almost more than she could bear. 'This mess is all *your* fault,' she told him grimly.

'My fault. . .?' He raised a dark, sardonic eyebrow, his lips twitching with amusement at the expression of anger and frustration on the girl's face.

'Of course it is!' she retorted waspishly, her normally generous lips tightening with annoyance and exasperation. 'If your telephone number hadn't been ex-directory, I could have contacted you on the phone, and saved myself a great deal of trouble.'

Xavier shrugged his broad shoulders. 'You may possibly be right,' he drawled blandly. 'On the other hand, maybe you should view the situation from my point of view? Perhaps one of the reasons I do not publicly disclose my phone number is simply that I wish

83

to avoid being disturbed—even by attractive women
such as yourself.'

Once again, as so often in their brief acquaintance,
Louisa found herself stunned by this man's overwhelming arrogance. Did he *really* believe that she'd braved
that awful storm just in the hope of seeing him again?
If so, his conceit was truly monumental!

'There's no need for you to have such a swollen head
on *my* account!' she ground out through clenched
teeth. 'I can assure you that the *only* reason I'm here
at all is that without my handbag I had no money, no
credit cards and no driving licence.'

'All of which are now quite safely back in your
hotel,' he pointed out smoothly.

'OK, OK. But I didn't know that, did I?' She glared
across the room at him. 'And if you think you're the
next best thing to a. . .a Venus fly-trap—you can think
again!' she added belligerently. 'Because even trying to
reach this place is an absolute nightmare. So anyone
wanting to see you *that* badly has to be totally and
utterly desperate to find a man!'

Clearly hoping to puncture his amazing arrogance,
she was completely nonplussed when Xavier threw
back his head and roared with laughter.

'Ah, Louisa—what a really enchanting girl you are!'
he grinned. 'I have been called many things in my
time—but *never* a "Venus fly-trap"!' And to her baffled
fury, he began to laugh again.

'I don't see that it's so damned funny!' she told him
with a scowl.

'No, of course it isn't,' he agreed blandly. But she
wasn't deceived. Even from across the room, she could
still see the deep gleam of amusement in his glittering
dark eyes.

'Well, if you think——'

Xavier quickly raised his hand. 'I think that you must
have misunderstood what I was saying earlier,' he told
her firmly. 'I am, in fact, enchanted to have your
company here today. After all, I seldom have the
opportunity of rescuing a damsel in distress. Neither
do I often have the pleasure of seeing such a beautiful

girl—clothed only in my dressing-gown!—sitting beside my own fireside!'

Oh, lord! How on earth was she supposed to respond to *that* remark? Louisa asked herself wildly. It was totally disconcerting the way this man could turn his amazing charm off and on, just like water from a tap.

Quickly tightening her belt, and nervously drawing the edges of the robe closer about her body, she desperately wished that she didn't feel quite so tongue-tied and awkward.

Xavier might be regarding her with a bland, almost disinterested expression on his face, but she knew—if only from the sardonic amusement glinting in his dark eyes—that he was perfectly well aware of her acute discomfiture. If only she really *was* the sort of sophisti-cated career woman he seemed to believe she repre-sented, she might be able to conduct this kind of frivolous, *risqué* conversation with a fluency and ease which, unfortunately, she didn't possess. Although she longed to say something totally crushing and annihil-ating, which would put him firmly in his place, her mind simply refused to co-operate, remaining obsti-nately blank and void.

She was rescued from her mounting confusion by a knock on the door, and the entry of the housekeeper, Rosa. The older woman clicked her tongue at the sight of the food, which remained virtually untouched, addressing a flood of incomprehensible words at both Xavier and Louisa as she crossed the room to collect the tray.

Maybe she really *had* lost her mind, Louisa thought, struggling to try to understand the plump woman's strange language. It seemed as though the housekeeper was having an argument with Xavier—and one which she eventually lost as she finally bowed to the com-manding tone of his voice. Giving a shrug of her shoulders, Rosa cast her eyes dramatically up at the ceiling, muttering under her breath as she left the room.

'I do hope your housekeeper wasn't too upset by my lack of appetite?' Louisa asked anxiously.

He gave a quick shake of his dark head. 'No. We were merely having a small discussion. About a completely different, private matter,' he added, with a dismissive wave of his hand.

Xavier's idea of a 'small discussion' seemed to consist of him laying down the law, and forcing others to accept what he said, Louisa thought ruefully. Making a mental note to avoid all 'discussions' like the plague, she murmured, 'I wasn't quite sure what she was saying, of course, but——'

'Rosa and her husband, Franco—who acts as my chauffeur—have always lived up here, in the mountains,' Xavier explained. 'As a consequence, they are more at home with their native Corsican dialect than with the French language. In fact,' he added with a shrug, 'I am told that it is not dissimilar to the Tuscan dialect of Italy.'

'I'm afraid that I don't speak Italian. But I did manage to understand one or two words. And, quite honestly. . .' Louisa gave a helpless shake of her head '. . . I think I must be losing my mind!'

'*Comment*. . .?'

Louisa hastened to explain. 'It wasn't until I heard Rosa mention the girl's name that I realised *just* what an idiot I've been.' She brushed a distracted hand through her long hair. 'I really do seem to have gone completely to pieces, lately!'

He frowned. 'I don't understand what you're talking about.'

'Oh, I'm sorry. I'm not making myself clear. I was referring to your niece—Marie-Thérèse. Where *is* she, by the way? Have you really got her locked up in a dungeon, here in this castle?'

'Of course not!' His dark frown deepened. 'Where did you get such a ridiculous idea?'

'It was just—er—just something my brother said. . .'

Xavier gave an angry snort of derision. 'Your brother is both a liar and a fool!' he snapped.

'Now—just a minute——!'

'For your information,' he continued coldly, ignoring

her protest 'I can tell you that Marie-Thérèse, and my aunt Sophie, have merely gone to stay with some relatives at Calvi, in the north of the island.'

'Yes, well. . .that sounds nice,' she muttered lamely, wishing to heavens that she'd kept her stupid mouth firmly shut. But Xavier was clearly not prepared to be deflected from the subject.

'I do not understand this reference to a "dungeon". Kindly explain yourself!'

'There's nothing to explain. It was just a silly, flip remark,' she told him hurriedly. 'You see, I understood from my stepbrother that you had insisted on your niece leaving Paris, that she was being kept here, at the castle, against her will.'

'*What nonsense!*' he exploded.

Despite his angry reaction, Louisa felt impelled to do what she could for the young girl.

'Well, I'm sorry, Xavier, but, whatever you think of my stepbrother, I can assure you that he really *was* worried about your niece. She apparently phoned him in London, saying that she was very unhappy. And. . . and before you start shouting at me again — or accusing my brother of lying,' Louisa added defiantly, as the stormy expression on his face suddenly became granite-hard and implacable, 'I can't think of any reason why Jamie should make up such an extraordinary story.'

For a moment she thought she'd gone too far. But when he didn't explode again with fury, as she had very much feared that he would, Louisa was so thankful to have avoided yet another full-blooded quarrel with this difficult man that she suggested tentatively, 'It is possible that it might be just a mistake on Jamie's part, isn't it? There may have been language difficulties. Maybe my stepbrother didn't fully understand what Marie-Thérèse was saying.'

Xavier regarded her sternly for a moment, before he gave a shrug of his broad shoulders. 'It is *just* possible, I suppose. However, I will have a long talk with my niece tomorrow, when she and my aunt return from

Calvi. We will then know exactly *who* is speaking the truth in this matter,' he added grimly.

Louisa flinched at the clear threat in his voice. She had no idea of what had been going on, but she was quite certain that Jamie had sounded genuinely upset by the young French girl's plea for help. However, even though she was ashamed of being so cowardly, Louisa could only thank her lucky stars that she would have left this castle, and wouldn't be around tomorrow to witness the confrontation between Xavier and his niece.

'Do you think it might be—um—a good idea if we changed the subject?' she asked hesitantly. 'I mean—er—maybe we could agree *not* to talk about either Jamie or Marie-Thérèse?'

Xavier shrugged, his lips twisted in a wry, sardonic smile. 'I, too, have become thoroughly bored by the subject. So, yes, by all means let us discard your stepbrother and my niece. In fact, I am much more interested in hearing about *you*,' he added smoothly, rising from his chair to come over and sit down on the sofa beside her.

'Me. . .?' She gave a breathless, shaky laugh. The close proximity of his tall, broad-shouldered figure was once again causing her heart to begin thudding painfully in her chest, and she gazed helplessly around the room, vainly seeking some avenue of escape.

However, beneath his calm, if probing questions about her background, she found herself gradually beginning to relax. Not that there was much to tell him, of course. However, Xavier did seem genuinely interested in hearing about her mother, who, having been left a young widow, had met and married a widower, Brian Kendall, with a son only two years younger than Louisa.

'And you all lived happily ever after?'

'Yes, indeed we did—for a while, anyway,' she assured Xavier, a small far-away smile playing on her lips as she recalled what now seemed the golden, sunny days of her childhood. A happy time, which had come to such an abrupt end when her stepfather, Brian, had died of a sudden and unexpected heart attack.

'My mother was desolate, of course.' Louisa sighed heavily. There seemed no way to adequately explain how her mother, seemingly losing all will to live without her husband, had quickly succumbed to a devouring cancer within nine months of his untimely death.

'So, you were left to raise your brother and to earn a living for you both?' he said, when she'd stumbled over the bare bones of the story.

She nodded. 'Yes. Unfortunately, I don't seem to have made a great success of bringing up Jamie, although he was sixteen years old, at the time.

'I know that we've agreed not to discuss the subject,' she added hastily. 'But I really do think that a lot of his problems are probably my fault. Maybe if I hadn't been quite so protective of him—always rescuing him from any trouble just in the nick of time—Jamie might have managed to stand on his own two feet, and grown up a lot sooner. To tell you the truth, I don't think that I did him any favours,' she murmured unhappily, staring blindly at the flickering logs in the large grate.

'It is easy to be wise after the event,' Xavier told her quietly, accompanying his words with a remarkably warm, genuine smile, before questioning her further on the progress of her career to date.

Remembering that she was talking to an extremely successful worldwide financier, who was unlikely to be interested in her brief career, Louisa confined herself to a short outline of her position with Frost, Gerard and Lumley.

'Unfortunately, I was in such a state last night, worried sick about my missing handbag, that I completely forgot to contact my office. Still, that was probably a good thing,' she added gloomily. 'Since you're now refusing to work with me, I'll probably find that I don't even have a job when I get back to London.'

'Nonsense—you clearly possess considerable talent for your work.'

'But not enough talent to do business with you — right?' she retorted bitterly.

'You are quite wrong,' he said firmly. 'My decision had nothing to do with your business ability.'

Louisa gave an unhappy shrug. 'Until I return to England, there's nothing I can do about the situation. Anyway, why should you care?' she added acidly. 'Compared to your international business, my career must seem totally uninteresting.'

'Not at all. One must begin somewhere, and you are still very young, of course,' he murmured, before questioning her more closely about the firm—and her relationship with Neville Frost.

Quite why Xavier should be so interested in both Neville and her company, she had no idea. However, she did her best to explain, haltingly at first and then more confidently, how, fresh out of secretarial college, she'd been determined to carve out a successful career for herself. Working long hours for little pay, in an effort to prove that she was capable of an executive position within the firm, her efforts had finally been rewarded with her appointment as private secretary and personal assistant to Neville Frost—the young grandson of one of the founders of the business.

'Neville is now one of the senior partners,' she told Xavier, adding with a shrug, 'but I don't think that he's ever going to make managing director. There's a lot of "dead wood" at the very top of the company. They're not likely to give up their cushy, well-paid jobs without a fight, certainly not for someone they regard as far too young and impetuous.'

Xavier nodded. 'It's a common story,' he agreed. But Louisa found herself becoming increasingly confused as he continued to probe into her relationship with Neville Frost. Why was he so interested in the young Englishman?

However, despite trying to stonewall Xavier's persistent, searching questions, she found herself eventually having to try to explain the situation.

'Well. . .' she sighed. 'I suppose it all comes down to

the fact that Neville is a workaholic — and so am I — which is probably the main basis of our friendship.'

'Friendship. . .?' he queried softly, raising a hand to lazily tuck a stray lock of hair behind her ear. 'Do you mean "friend" — as in "lover"?'

'No — I do *not*!' she snapped tersely, inching nervously back against the cushions of the sofa.

This conversation appeared to be going completely off the rails. And to have him sitting so close to her on this large sofa — one designed to seat at least four people in comfort — was definitely *not* a good idea!

She and Xavier had seemed to be getting on so much better. But with her skin still feeling scorched from the brief touch of his warm fingers, and the increasingly loud beating of her heart — now pounding like a sledge-hammer in her ears — Louisa could feel the whole situation rapidly spinning out of her control. The combination of this man's Gallic charm and over-whelming sex appeal was absolutely *lethal*!

'So — you are not lovers?'

'Not that it's any of your business — but no, we don't have that sort of relationship,' she muttered, desperately trying to think of something — anything! — which would turn this dangerous subject back on to a much safer course.

But Xavier seemed unstoppable.

'I still do not yet understand the extent of your friendship with this Englishman,' he queried smoothly. 'Especially since I do not believe it is possible for a man and a woman to have a friendship which is completely devoid of all sexual interest.'

'That. . .that's absolutely ridiculous!' she protested breathlessly. 'Besides, quite apart from anything else, the relationship between Neville and myself isn't based on *that* sort of foundation at all.'

Xavier shrugged. 'I freely admit that I've never under-stood the English attitude to *l'amour*. However, I gather from what you've just said that you are maybe planning to marry this man some time in the future. . .? It sounds a very strange, odd situation,' he drawled slowly, gazing steadily down into her green eyes. 'For instance, I ask myself, why should this very lovely, beautiful girl wish to become the wife of a man who — quite astonishingly! — does not appear to find her sexually attractive?'

'I didn't say that!' Louisa retorted quickly.

'But surely you must see that there is no logic in this situation,' Xavier drawled coolly. 'If this man, Neville does *not* find you attractive — then he is clearly a fool. If, on the other hand, he *is* attracted to you, but has done nothing about it, then he is equally foolish. . .yes?'

Louisa closed her eyes for a moment, desperately trying to prod her tired brain into some form of logical reply — preferably one which would put a stop to Xavier's persistent and embarrassing questions. But her mind seemed to be bogged down in a sticky mass of confusion, obviously disintegrating under the stress and strain of the last few days. Why else should she be possessed of the most extraordinary and almost overwhelming urge to rest her tired head against his strong shoulder, or to feel the strength of his arms about her weary body?

'In my country, of course, there is no such problem,' Xavier was saying as she struggled to pull herself together. 'We French understand a *mariage de convenance.*'

'You do?' Louisa's eyelashes fluttered nervously as she stared up at the man, who now seemed to be looming even closer over her shrinking figure.

'Yes, of course,' he drawled smoothly. 'But I cannot understand why you should wish to throw yourself away — and on a man who, if I may say so, sounds remarkably boring.'

'Neville *isn't* boring!' she protested weakly, her cheeks reddening as Xavier gave a low, mocking laugh. 'And. . .and I think that it's about time we changed the subject,' she added as firmly as she could. 'I'm sure the storm must be over by now, and if Rosa has managed to dry my clothes —— '

'No, I don't think so.'

Louisa gave a heavy sigh. 'Well, even if my clothes are still wringing wet, I'm sure that you must have *something* I can wear.'

'I have no idea whether the storm is still raging — or about the state of your clothing.' He gave a shrug of his broad shoulders. 'I am merely saying that I am not yet prepared to let you leave this castle.'

'Oh, for heaven's sake!' She gritted her teeth. 'I want to go — right this minute! In fact, I demand —— '

His sardonic laugh cut across her words. 'You demand. . .what? That I kiss you?'

'*No!*'

'But yes!' he mocked. 'It is obvious that you have been wanting me to kiss you for the past hour.'

'*What*. . .? How d-dare you suggest such a thing?' she spluttered, her cheeks flushing hectically beneath the gleam in his glittering dark eyes, as his arms began closing slowly about her.

'Why deny the truth, Louisa?' he murmured softly, taking no notice of her attempt to wriggle free of his embrace. 'Especially when *I*, too, have been fighting a strong urge to kiss you — ever since the moment you arrived here, earlier this afternoon.'

'But you can't — you m-mustn't. . .!' she gasped as his dark head came down towards her. Her pulses seemed to be racing wildly out of control, and it suddenly felt as if iron bands were clamped tightly about her chest, making it almost impossible for her to breathe properly.

'Oh, yes, I can!' he murmured huskily, ignoring her stammered protest as his arms closed firmly about her slim figure. 'And, indeed, it seems that I must. . .!' he added thickly, staring down at the dazed green eyes and flushed cheeks of the girl lying beneath him, the long tendrils of hair flowing like liquid, fiery gold over the deep red silk cushions.

Louisa shivered with helpless excitement, her gaze held and trapped by the steely, determined gleam in his glittering dark eyes. She could almost tangibly feel a deep surge of blood beginning to rage swiftly through her veins. All her senses seemed to be at fever pitch — her nostrils filled with the aromatic scent of his musky cologne, her ears only aware of the sound of his uneven breath, and the hurried, pounding beat of his heart so close to her own.

'This is m-madness. . .' she whispered helplessly.

'Yes, I know,' he agreed softly—and then any further protest was lost beneath the ruthless possession of his lips.

His mouth was hard and firm, and as her lips parted beneath the forceful pressure she desperately tried to cling on to sanity, to remember how she feared and distrusted this hard, difficult and cruelly arrogant man, who—with one simple phone call—had almost certainly wrecked her professional career. But her own weak senses were betraying her. Almost faint with dizziness, she found herself spinning helplessly down into a deep, dark swirling pool of desire.

Responding mindlessly to the powerful, sensual spell of his seductive lips and tongue, she seemed to hear a strange roaring noise in her ears as she became hopelessly consumed by an overwhelming, driving force over which she had no control. And as his kiss deepened, she became oblivious of everything except the deep, loud thud of his heartbeat, hammering in unison with her own, and the hard strength of the long, muscular body pinning her so fiercely down on to the thick cushions of the sofa.

Dazed and helpless with passion, she was barely aware of voicing a small, helpless moan as his lips slowly left hers, his mouth trailing a scorching path down the smooth length of her neck to the soft skin at the base of her throat.

'Louisa!' he muttered thickly, his breathing ragged and uneven as she felt his long, tanned, warm fingers loosening the belt of her robe. 'It seems you have bewitched me. But I. . .I cannot help myself,' he added huskily, before drawing aside the towelling gown, and pressing his lips to the softly scented cleft between her breasts.

Dazed with passion, a hapless prisoner of the overwhelmingly intense, physical sensations aroused by the seductive touch of his hands and mouth on her bare, quivering flesh, she could only moan with helpless pleasure and delight as he impatiently brushed the robe back off her shoulders. For a long moment his dark eyes, glittering with arousal, absorbed the pearly sheen of her pale alabaster skin. And then, with a deep groan, he lowered his head again, his mouth moving hungrily and possessively over the silky softness of her full breasts.

Drowning in a vortex of erotic, sensual passion, Louisa no longer knew nor even cared whether she was being betrayed by her weak emotions. With thrilling shock-waves of overwhelming desire and passion now spiralling violently through her body, nothing seemed more important or urgent than the compulsive, driving need to wantonly respond to the throbbing frenzy of excitement, which appeared to have her in thrall. And then, with shocking suddenness, the silence of the large room was abruptly shattered.

'*Oncle*? Yoo-hoo. . . We're back. . .'

At the sound of the young voice, Xavier quickly raised his head, his tanned features still hard and taut with arousal as he cursed violently under his breath.

Jerked so abruptly back to reality, it was some moments before Louisa's confused, dazed mind was able to understand why Xavier — his dark eyes glittering with rage and fury — was hurriedly pulling the edges of her towelling gown together. But, as her ears absorbed the echoing sound of quick, sharp footsteps on the stone flags outside in the passage, she could feel the blood draining from her face when the heavy oak door of the room was thrown open.

'I can't think *why* you're so anxious to see my uncle, Désirée,' a girl was saying with barely concealed impatience, before giving a muffled shriek. 'Ah — *mon Dieu*! I — er — I'm sorry, Uncle. I didn't mean to. . . I didn't realise. . .' Her voice trailed nervously away.

In the long, embarrassed silence which followed, the couple — who were still helplessly entwined on the sofa — found themselves beneath the startled gaze of three women, the expression on their astonished, stunned faces conveying varying degrees of what could only be described as shock, horror and dismay.

CHAPTER SEVEN

SITTING huddled on the edge of the bed, with her face buried in her hands, Louisa almost groaned out loud with despair. She would happily have given just about everything she possessed if, by some miracle, she could have found herself immediately transported back to the safe and secure haven of her own apartment, in London.

Never, in all her life, had she known such a *hideously* embarrassing situation! In fact, the words 'shock, horror and dismay' would hardly even begin to describe adequately the ghastly mess in which she now found herself.

Still shivering with reaction to the scene downstairs, when she and Xavier had been discovered so closely entwined on the sofa, Louisa could feel herself growing hot and cold, her cheeks burning with shame and humiliation.

Unfortunately, still dazed and completely disorientated from Xavier's lovemaking, she'd been able to do no more than huddle in a corner of the large sofa, tightly wrapping her arms around her stunned, trembling figure like a badly frightened child. Shivering almost uncontrollably as the heat of frenzied desire quickly drained away from her quivering body, leaving her feeling totally bereft and on the verge of tears, she'd only been dimly aware of Xavier's gallant reaction to the crisis. Swiftly jumping to his feet, and placing himself so as to shield her from the others' gaze, he'd angrily demanded an explanation for the sudden intrusion.

It was some time before Louisa, drowning in abject misery, had managed to pull herself together—only to find that she was caught up in the midst of an extremely acrimonious family quarrel.

She had no doubts about its being a family row, since

TAKE 4 LOVE ON CALL ROMANCES FREE

Mills & Boon Love on Call romances capture all the excitement, intrigue and emotion of a busy medical world. But a world never too busy to ignore love and romance.

We will send you four Love on Call romances plus a cuddly teddy and a mystery gift absolutely FREE, as your introduction to this superb series.

At the same time we'll reserve a subscription for you to our Reader Service. Every month you could receive the latest four Love on Call romances delivered direct to your door postage and packing FREE, plus our FREE Newsletter packed with author news, competitions, special offers and much more.

What's more, there's no obligation. You may cancel or suspend your subscription at any time. So you've nothing to lose and a whole world of romance to gain!

YOUR GIFT

Return this card today and we'll send you this lovely cuddly teddy bear absolutely FREE.

Fill in the Free Books Certificate overleaf ▼▼

Free Books Certificate

Yes! Please send me four FREE Love on Call romances together with my FREE cuddly teddy and mystery gift. Please also reserve a special Reader Service subscription for me. If I decide to subscribe, I shall receive four brand new books every month for just £7.20, postage and packing FREE. If I decide not to subscribe, I shall write to you within 10 days. Any free books and gifts will be mine to keep in any case. I understand that I am under no obligation whatsoever - I may cancel or suspend my subscription at any time simply by writing to you. I am over 18 years of age.

Your Extra Bonus Gift

We all love mysteries, so as well as the books and cuddly teddy we've an intriguing gift just for you. No clues - send off today!

1A4D

Ms/Mrs/Miss/Mr _____

Address _____

_____

_____

Postcode _____ Signature _____

Mills & Boon
Reader Service
FREEPOST
PO Box 236
Croydon
CR9 9EL

▲ Send No Money Now

it quickly became obvious that two of the three women could only be Xavier's elderly aunt Sophie, accompanied by his young niece, Marie-Thérèse. But it had taken some minutes before the mist had finally cleared from Louisa's stunned mind, and she'd realised that she had already met the third member of the trio. There could be no mistaking the glamorous dark-haired woman, Désirée, who'd been so rude to her in Xavier's office on the day of her arrival in Corsica.

However, it soon became clear to Louisa that if she thought she'd seen Xavier in a bad temper before, it was as *nothing* to the cold rage and fury with which he was now confronting the three women.

'Ça alors, Tante. . .!' he growled menacingly, before icily demanding to know what she and Marie-Thérèse were doing back here, at the castle. Surely they hadn't been expected to return before tomorrow?

With his aunt and Marie-Thérèse both speaking loudly and at once, as they hastened to explain their unexpected arrival, Louisa's already confused mind rapidly began to feel numb and battered amid all the bedlam. However, despite having difficulty in keeping up with the rapid stream of words—both aunt and niece noisily interrupting one another—she eventually gathered that the trip had been organised by Xavier's aunt Sophie. Thrilled to have Marie-Thérèse staying for a while at the castle, the elderly woman had enjoyed arranging a busy social whirl for the young girl. Following an invitation to spend a few days with some distant cousins—who were also intending to throw a large party to welcome Marie-Thérèse—Xavier's chauffeur had driven them to Calvi, in the north-east of the island.

'Kindly do not try my patience too far, Tante!' Xavier ground out harshly. 'I already know all about the arrangements for your visit to Calvi. However, I am *still* waiting to hear why you have returned home a day early. Is this your doing, Marie-Thérèse?' he added, his ominous growl producing a swift denial from the young girl.

'No, it certainly isn't!' she retorted. 'In fact, as far as

I'm concerned, I was having a really great time with my cousins. Especially when we were taken on a visit to the ancient Citadelle. It's a really amazing place!' she added enthusiastically. 'After touring the ramparts, we went to see the ruins of the house where Christopher Columbus was born. Although, to tell the truth——' she shrugged '—I'm not sure that he was born in Calvi—most people seem to believe that he actually came from Genoa. But I like to think that he *was* Corsican, because he's a *much* more interesting person than boring old Napoléon, and——'

'Marie-Thérèse! That is *not* what I want to hear. Kindly keep to the point!' Xavier ground out through clenched teeth.

'OK—OK. Keep your hair on!' she retorted with a cheeky grin, clearly the only one present who was prepared to stand up to her formidable guardian. 'Anyway, as I said, we were having a really good time,' his niece continued. 'And, quite frankly, I was in no hurry to return. But Désirée, who was also at the party, kept on going on and *on* about how we ought to be getting back here to the castle.'

Despite her confused state of mind, it was obvious to Louisa that there was clearly no love lost between Xavier's niece and Désirée. Glancing with dislike at the dark, sultry-looking woman standing beside her, Marie-Thérèse quickly proceeded to throw the other woman to the wolves.

'In fact,' the young girl continued, 'it's *all* Désirée's fault! It was *she* who persuaded Tante Sophie that it would be easy for her to give us a lift back here *and* save you having to send Franco to pick us up. But, if you want to know what *I* think,' his niece added cattily, '*I* think that she just wanted to keep a beady eye on you!'

'When I want to hear your opinion, I'll ask for it,' Xavier told her icily, before turning his cold, steely gaze on Désirée. 'Well. . .? What have you to say on this matter?'

Only too thankful that she wasn't standing in the other woman's elegant small shoes, Louisa found herself recoiling as Désirée threw both her and Marie-Thérèse a venomous glance of pure hatred, before quickly turning to give Xavier a warm, sensual smile.

'Ah, *chéri*. . .' she murmured, moving quickly across the room to place a fluttering hand on his arm. 'Please don't be mad with little me,' she pouted, gazing beseechingly up at him with a helpless flutter of her long black eyelashes. 'I was only trying to be helpful.'

'Oh, really. . .?' he drawled, his lips tightening into a thin line.

'But yes — of course I was.' Désirée smiled mistily up at him, looking more enchantingly weak and fragile by the minute as, apparently about to collapse any moment, she clung helplessly to his tall figure.

Xavier gave a snort of irritation as he firmly removed her hands from his arm. 'Unfortunately, *madame*, I do not find it at all "helpful" to have you interfering with my family arrangements in this way.'

'But. . .*chéri!*' she cried. 'How *can* you talk to me like this? Especially when we have meant so much to each other.'

'Don't be so stupid, Désirée,' he snapped with increasing irritation. 'And as for you. . .' He turned menacingly on his niece, who was grinning with broad enjoyment at the scene in front of her. 'You can take that smile off your face right this minute!'

Clearly hoping to calm down the increasingly tense atmosphere, Aunt Sophie hastened to intervene.

'Xavier, my dear boy — don't you feel that you are perhaps making *too* much of this unfortunate situation?' she ventured nervously. 'After all, what can a day matter, one way or another? And how could we possibly have known that you were — um — that we would find you — er. . .' The elderly woman's voice faltered for a moment as her nephew turned his angry gaze in her direction.

'It's no use glaring at me like that!' she continued defensively. 'You may be upset and embarrassed by what has happened — but so, I can assure you, are we. Really, you know, this is *not* the sort of — er — well, this whole situation is definitely not at all *comme il*

faut! In fact,' she continued bravely, her cheeks reddening in the face of his baleful silence, 'I have to say
that I am *deeply* shocked by what I have seen here
today. How could you, whom I've always thought of as
such a gentleman, be behaving in so disgraceful a
manner? And in your own sitting-room! Surely this
castle has enough bedrooms,' she added querulously.
'I really can't understand how——'

'*Tais-toi, Tante*!'

Everyone flinched nervously as Xavier's bellow of
rage and fury thundered around the room. In the
ensuing silence, he took a deep breath before firmly
taking control of the situation.

'Marie-Thérèse, kindly take Louisa upstairs to your
bedroom and find her some clothes to wear,' he
ordered brusquely, before firmly informing his aunt
that he had no wish to detain her any further—a barely
disguised order to leave the room with which the
elderly woman hastily agreed.

How Louisa managed to force her trembling figure
off the sofa and across the large room towards the
door, she had no idea. As she trailed silently up the
stairs behind Marie-Thérèse, there hadn't seemed anything she could say to the young French girl which was
likely to improve the already fraught situation.

Left alone while Marie-Thérèse disappeared into an
adjoining dressing-room to find something for her to
wear, Louisa slumped down on to the girl's bed. Maybe
it was a reaction to the scene downstairs, but there
seemed little she could do to stop herself from shivering
almost uncontrollably. How *could* she have been so
foolish? What on earth had possessed her to let Xavier
make love to her? Especially when it could have meant
little or nothing to such an experienced, sophisticated
man of the world. She didn't even *dare* begin to wonder
what he must think of her. After the way she'd so
easily responded to his touch, she couldn't blame him
for concluding that she was obviously what the
Americans called 'an easy lay'. How he must despise
her! But no more than she despised herself, Louisa
thought, tears coming to her eyes as she realised that it

was far too late to stop herself from falling in love with Xavier—because she already had.

'Here you are. I hope everything fits.'

Louisa looked up, startled, as Marie-Thérèse bounced back into the room, her arms full of garments. Feeling deeply embarrassed and wishing the earth could suddenly swallow her up, she found herself helplessly mumbling, 'I really am very grateful. . . It's very kind of you. . .'

'Not at all,' Marie-Thérèse told her breezily. 'As I expect you know, a request from my uncle is, in reality, nothing more than a direct command!' She grinned over her shoulder, the smile dying on her lips as she gazed with concern at the pale face and hunched, shivering figure of the English girl. 'Are you feeling all right?'

'Yes, yes, I'm fine,' Louisa muttered, staring fixedly down at the fingers twisting themselves nervously in her lap.

'Did you get caught in the storm? We were lucky to miss it, but it can be a bit frightening up here in the mountains,' Marie-Thérèse said, picking up a pair of jeans and holding them against her figure as she gazed into a nearby mirror. 'I really think you're going to be too tall for these,' she added, turning back to throw them on to the bed. 'You're English, aren't you? Are you on holiday here in Corsica?'

'Yes. . .no. . . I mean, I came over here on business, really. But I also had to see your uncle. . .on a family matter. . .' Her voice trailed away. How could she possibly explain everything to this young girl? The situation had by now become so complicated that even she herself was finding it difficult to understand what had happened.

Marie-Thérèse turned to look at her in surprise. 'I didn't know we had any family in England.'

Louisa gave a helpless shrug. 'No, well—it's more to do with *my* family,' she muttered evasively.

'Really?' The other girl gazed at her expectantly, but when Louisa continued to stare blindly down at her tightly clenched hands she added, 'I know I'm being nosy — but I'm dying to know what's going on. After all — ' she grinned ' — it's not every day that I discover my oh, so strict, morally upright uncle having a romp on the sofa with one of his girlfriends!'

'It wasn't like that!' Louisa protested quickly, before swiftly reminding herself that she could hardly blame Marie-Thérèse. It *would* have been just a 'romp' to Xavier. And she was obviously just his latest conquest — merely a fresh addition to the long, long list of his girlfriends.

Louisa buried her face in her hands. 'It's all Jamie's fault! If it hadn't been for you and my brother, I'd *never* be in such a mess!' she moaned helplessly, before immediately regretting her wild outburst. It wasn't fair to take her feelings of acute distress and misery out on this young girl, even if her brief affair with Jamie was the cause of all Louisa's present problems.

Marie-Thérèse stared at her in wide-eyed astonishment. 'Jamie. . .? James Kendall? He is your brother?'

Louisa nodded, sighing heavily as she realised that there was no way she could escape either from this castle, or from having to tell Marie-Thérèse exactly *why* she was in Corsica.

'It's a long and complicated story, I'm afraid,' she began, before explaining that she was James Kendall's stepsister, and relating all that had happened following Jamie's panic-stricken phone call, some weeks ago, which had led to her first encounter with the girl's uncle — and the confusion that had arisen over Xavier's use of the title Comte Cinarchesi, which he used when visiting Corsica.

'It's been a complete and total muddle from beginning to end,' Louisa told her with an unhappy shrug of her slim shoulders. 'I might have been able to sort the matter out if it had just been a personal one, concerning you and my stepbrother,' she added with a sigh. 'But trying to do business with your uncle as well just made things far too complicated. I suppose, if I'm honest, it really was the right, sensible decision for him to refuse to have any financial dealings with me. Unfortunately, I don't think my boss is going to be

very happy about what's happened. In fact——' she
gave another weary sigh, '—I'm almost certain to find
that I've lost my job when I get back to London.'

'Oh, Louisa—how awful! I'm so sorry. . . I had no
idea of the problems I've caused,' Marie-Thérèse
exclaimed, hurriedly sitting down beside Louisa and
putting her arm about the other girl's bowed shoulders.
'I really am sorry to have caused so much trouble.'

'It was your phone call, you see,' Louisa muttered
unhappily. 'Jamie really was very upset and worried
about you. He said that it sounded as though you were
being kept a prisoner here in the castle.'

'Oh, no!' The other girl jumped quickly to her feet,
pacing with agitation up and down over the thick pale
pink carpet, designed to complement the *toile de Jouy*
pink and white wallpaper and matching curtains, in a
room clearly designed for a young girl.

But Marie-Thérèse was clearly no longer a child,
Louisa reminded herself as the French girl paced
restlessly up and down the room, her hands nervously
clasped to cheeks red with embarrassment. With her
light brown hair cut in a smart bob, and her slim figure
clothed in a simple if expensive skirt and matching
sweater, which bore an indefinable air of Parisian chic,
Marie-Thérèse was clearly a very attractive young
woman.

'It's all my fault! How could I have been *so*
stupid. . .?' the girl was muttering unhappily to herself,
before she took a deep breath and turned around to
face Louisa. 'I seem to have caused a great deal of
trouble to you, poor Jamie and my uncle,' she admitted
sadly. 'I never thought, you see, of the consequences
of my phone call. I was just so unhappy and miserable. . .' She brushed a distraught hand through her
hair.

Louisa frowned in puzzlement. 'I really don't understand the problem. I mean, your uncle doesn't seem to
think that you are pregnant, so——'

'*Enceinte*? Do you mean that you thought I was
expecting a baby?' The girl stared at her in astonishment. 'Of course I'm not pregnant!'

'Then why is your uncle insisting that you and Jamie must be married?'

'What. . .?' Marie-Thérèse cried, her horrified shriek of dismay echoing around the room as she sank limply down on to the bed. 'I simply *don't* believe it!' she wailed. 'Uncle has never said anything to me about this crazy idea. What on earth is going on?'

Louisa grimaced and gave a helpless shrug of her shoulders. 'I think you'd better tell me your side of the story, right from the beginning. And then, maybe, we can both try and find a solution to this mess.'

Amid all the self-recriminations and disjointed words of regret from the conscience-stricken girl, it was some time before Louisa was able to put together the bare bones of the unhappy story. Obviously deeply embarrassed, Marie-Thérèse eventually confessed that she had behaved stupidly during her phone call to Jamie. 'I was just so *mad* with my uncle,' she explained, her voice rising in anger as she related what lay behind her apparent cry for help. In essence, it appeared that she normally lived with her uncle, Xavier, in his very large and grand apartment in Paris. According to the girl, the Parc Monceau was definitely *the* place to live in the *huitième* district of the city; she also appeared to feel that it was definitely '*le plus chic*' to have her very own luxurious suite of rooms within the huge apartment.

Reading between the lines, Louisa came to the conclusion that Xavier was a very generous and indulgent if somewhat stuffy uncle. His only fault, it seemed, lay in the fact that he'd totally failed to realise that Marie-Thérèse was no longer a child. Taking his responsibilities as a guardian very seriously, he'd monitored her comings and goings with increasing vigilance, which had led to his niece becoming increasingly fed up and frustrated. 'But Uncle Xavier has been very good to me, and of course I have no money of my own,' she added with a slight shrug, explaining that it was a serious consideration for a young girl with no money, who wished to enjoy herself in Paris. 'So I used to slip out late at nights, to meet my friends and go to nightclubs.'

'Without your uncle knowing anything about your activities, I take it?'

'Exactly!' The girl gave Louisa a grin which was so infectious that she found herself smiling back, before quickly reminding herself that there was nothing amusing about the situation.

'And I suppose that, as always happens, you eventually got caught,' she murmured.

Marie-Thérèse gave an unhappy nod. 'Yes. Uncle was waiting for me when I returned from a party, in the early hours of the morning,' she admitted with a sigh. Apparently, it hadn't been Xavier's anger which she had found so disturbing, since she'd always expected him to be furious if and when he eventually discovered what she'd been up to. It was his demand to know exactly *where* and with *whom* she'd been that evening which lay behind the whole sorry mess.

Marie-Thérèse had, it seemed, been out with a young rising executive in her uncle's business. Unfortunately, the person in question was also a happily married man. And knowing that her uncle would be furious, and possibly likely to sack the man from his job, she'd hoped to distract Xavier by saying that it was Jamie with whom she'd been out for the evening.

'I was just frightened — in a panic — so I said the first name that came into my head.' The girl waved her hands helplessly in the air. 'It never occurred to me. . . I mean, Jamie lived in London, and so I was sure he would be quite safe from my uncle's anger. I couldn't possibly have guessed that he would be so unreasonable . . .make *such* a fuss. . .' Marie-Thérèse groaned, tears welling up in her eyes as she at last realised the full consequences of her actions.

'So, having thrown poor Jamie to the wolves, what happened next?' Louisa demanded, feeling like shaking the girl who was now sobbing miserably beside her.

'He kept going on and on — and I was getting more and more frightened that he would find out about the man who worked in his office. I *really* didn't want to break up the man's marriage,' the girl muttered tearfully, before finally admitting that under the interrog-

ation she'd told Xavier everything she knew about
Jamie Kendall—including the fact that he was engaged
to be married to the daughter of an old business
acquaintance of her uncle, Lord Armstrong.

'I should have known—I should have remembered
that my uncle *never* forgets an injury, that once he has
made up his mind he is totally inflexible,' the girl
muttered dismally. 'You've *no* idea of just how tough
my uncle can be!'

Oh, yes I have! Louisa thought grimly as the other
girl explained how, barely giving her time to pack a
suitcase, Xavier had dragged her off to this mountain-
top castle in Corsica.

'That's when I rang your brother,' she explained.
'We'd only just arrived, and I was so unhappy and
confused that I. . .well, I just had to talk to *someone*.
But I do now see that it was very wrong of me,' she
added, casting a nervous, contrite glance at Louisa's
stern expression. 'Especially since my aunt has turned
out to be so kind and welcoming. Even my uncle has
taken a lot of trouble to make sure that I'm having a
nice holiday—and he's never mentioned the subject
since we left Paris. In fact,' she added, wiping away a
tear and fiercely blowing her nose, 'I really thought
that he'd forgotten all about our quarrel.'

Struggling into jeans which, as Marie-Thérèse had
forecast, were far too short for her tall figure, Louisa
was surprised to find herself feeling a deep pang of
sympathy for Xavier. It couldn't have been much fun
trying to look after a headstrong young teenager. In
fact, why he hadn't already murdered his tiresome
niece, she had no idea! Because, despite all the tears,
and deep apologies for having caused so many problems, the girl was now happily narrating, in graphic
detail, just what a wonderful time she'd been having in
Corsica.

'We're going to Bastia tomorrow,' she announced
with a smile. 'You'll love it! It has *such* a pretty port,
and the whole town is a marvellous mixture of new and
old buildings. I haven't been back there for a few years,
but I used to love the market stalls in the Place de

l'Hôtel-de-Ville,' she continued enthusiastically. 'They sold home-made wine, smoked sausages and ham, and there was a butcher who hung the head and skin of a wild boar outside his store. Wild boar is one of the delicacies of the island,' she pointed out as Louisa gave an involuntary exclamation of horror. 'What's wrong? Are you a vegetarian?'

'No, I'm not,' Louisa snapped. This girl was absolutely amazing! Didn't she have *any* idea of the trouble she'd caused? It was about time somebody brought her sharply down to earth. 'Just what are you intending to do about the marriage your uncle has planned for you?'

'Oh, come on! That's *such* a stupid idea; I can't possibly take it seriously!' Marie-Thérèse gave a nervous giggle of laughter. 'Even my uncle couldn't be *that* stuffy—not in this day and age.'

'Those are exactly the words I used, when we last discussed the matter. However, I can tell you that your uncle Xavier didn't take one blind bit of notice,' Louisa told her grimly. 'In fact, we had a *very* nasty row, and, as far as I can tell, he still hasn't changed his mind.'

Marie-Thérèse frowned over the tall English girl, who had abandoned her search for a bra to fit her full-breasted figure, and was now pulling a powder-blue cashmere sweater down over her head. 'But you weren't. . . I mean, you didn't seem to be *exactly* having a row with my uncle, when we arrived earlier this afternoon.'

Louisa could feel her face blushing a fiery red. 'Yes—um—well, things just got a bit out of control, that's all,' she muttered helplessly. 'I don't usually. . . I mean, it's not what you think,' she added lamely, desperately anxious to escape from the bright, inquisitive eyes of the young girl. And as soon as she got away from both this castle and Xavier, the better.

'Well, you've certainly put a spoke in Désirée's wheel!' Marie-Thérèse laughed gleefully. 'Her husband ran off and left her without any money, so she's had her eye on my uncle for some time. In fact, Tante Sophie and I were getting quite worried, because if they get married she'll turn Tante out of the castle, *tout de suite*! You'd better watch out,' the girl warned her. 'Désirée can be an absolute bitch — and she has a really filthy temper.'

'It sounds as if she and your uncle are ideally matched!' Louisa muttered sourly, quickly picking up a brush from the dressing-table, and dragging it roughly through her long hair.

She was certain that she'd never felt quite so miserable and unhappy in her life. She had *got* to get out of this awful place. Busy trying to recall the timetable of the ferries which ran daily back and forth to Nice — from where she could easily catch a plane to London — Louisa realised that she had missed some of what the other girl was saying.

'He's never recovered from the death of Georgette, of course. It all happened so long ago, and I hardly remember her — only that she was the most beautiful woman I've ever seen. Everyone says that my uncle was completely devastated when she was killed in the car crash, driving down the mountain,' Marie-Thérèse added sorrowfully. 'I don't think he's ever seriously looked at another woman. Or not until Désirée started coming around, pestering the life out of him. So, if he *has* taken a shine to you, that can only be good news!' She grinned. 'Are you in love with my uncle, Louisa?'

'Certainly not!' She retorted, quickly turning away to hide the deep red tell-tale flush staining her cheeks.

'Well, you definitely looked *very* loving on the sofa this afternoon! I thought Tante was going to have a heart attack!' the girl laughed. 'And you should have seen Désirée's face — the steam was practically coming out of her ears!'

'Can't we talk about anything else?' Louisa groaned, desperate to put a halt to this conversation.

'I was only putting off the evil moment.' Marie-Thérèse gave a heavy sigh. 'However, if I'm going to have to face the music, I suppose I'd better go down and get it over with.'

Wildly trying to think of some means of instant escape from the situation in which she found herself, Louisa slowly followed Marie-Thérèse downstairs. But, as they approached the large sitting-room, they could clearly hear a voice raised in anger on the other side of the door.

'It sounds as though Désirée is being horrid to poor old Tante Sophie,' Marie-Thérèse muttered grimly, before marching determinedly into the room.

'What's going on?' she demanded, surveying the flushed faces of the two older women, who were the room's only occupants. 'And where is my uncle?'

'He had to take a phone call. . .in his office,' her great-aunt told her, sinking wearily down into a chair. 'He's *very* angry with us. I do wish you hadn't persuaded me to return early, Désirée. Then there would have been no need for all this——'

'Nonsense! How many times do I have to tell you that I was only trying to be a good neighbour?' the glamorous woman protested angrily, clearly having lost a good deal of her cool self-possession while they had been out of the room. 'It's all her fault!' she added, pointing a trembling finger at Louisa's shrinking figure. 'There was no problem—not until that. . .that *disgusting* English girl suddenly appeared on the scene!'

Marie-Thérèse bristled, striding purposefully across the room towards the petite divorcee. 'You can say what you like about me—but you've no right to be so rude about a stranger, who is also a guest in our house.'

'How else should I describe a girl who is discovered practically *naked* in the arms of a man? And in the *salon*—of all places!' Désirée screeched, her temper by now well out of control.

'Although I'm sorry to have to agree with Désirée, she does have a point,' Tante Sophie intervened nervously. 'It was very wrong of Xavier. I never thought that he was the sort of man to be guilty of seducing young girls, or of behaving so dishonourably.'

'It is *she* who is the seductress!' Désirée yelled, jabbing a finger in the air towards Louisa, who was feeling completely dazed and shaken by the unexpected attack. 'It is *she* who has lost and betrayed her honour!'

'Oh, for heaven's sake!' Marie-Thérèse exploded. 'I'm fed up with all this business of "honour". It's

totally ridiculous, about a hundred years out of date—
and has absolutely *nothing* to do with the modern
world.' She gave a snort of angry laughter. 'From the
way you're all going on, anyone would think that
Louisa has been somehow seduced and ruined by my
uncle! But she's been no more "ruined" by what has
happened than *I* was by my brief love-affair with Jamie
Kendall.'

Désirée glared at the girl. 'How can you even *say*
such a thing? Have you no shame?' she hissed. 'I now
see that your uncle is quite right to insist on your
immediate marriage to this man.'

'Oh, really. . .?' Marie-Thérèse drawled slowly, and
Louisa was strongly reminded of the girl's formidable
guardian. 'Are you accusing my uncle Xavier of double
standards—of having one set of morals for the members of his family, and quite another for himself?'

'What nonsense is this?'

'Well, you can't have it both ways,' the girl pointed
out with a malicious grin. 'If I have been dishonoured
by Monsieur Kendall—then it would seem that my
uncle is equally guilty of dishonourable conduct
towards Louisa!'

Désirée, who was facing the open door, suddenly
gave a shrill, high-pitched laugh. 'Ah, Xavier! I didn't
see you standing in the doorway,' she cried, nervously
smoothing a hand over her long black hair. 'We were—
er—just having a little talk.'

Xavier didn't say anything as he walked slowly into
the room, all eyes focussed on him as he took a deep
breath and drew himself up to his full height.

'It seems that I must be grateful to my niece for
pointing out the serious defects and faults in my own
behaviour. There is, of course, only one right and
proper solution to this problem. Mademoiselle Thomas
and I must be married, immediately!'

CHAPTER EIGHT

LOUISA gave a heavy sigh, staring wide-eyed at the shafts of brilliant silvery moonlight flooding in through the arched Gothic windows of the bedroom.

As she restlessly tossed and turned in a state of almost perpetual motion, the long night seemed endless. And yet, only a few hours ago, she had fallen on this wide and comfortable bed in one of the many guest suites of the castle in a state of complete exhaustion, certain that she'd only to close her eyes before sinking into a deep and dreamless sleep. Unfortunately, despite the peaceful silence and luxurious comfort of her surroundings, she had found it impossible to gain any relief from the agitated, feverish turmoil of alarm and confusion swirling through her weary brain.

With another heavy sigh of deep depression, Louisa gave up the unequal battle, stretching out a weary arm to switch on a bedside lamp. Yawning with tiredness and fatigue, she plumped up the soft pillows in an effort to make herself more comfortable, before leaning back and brushing the tangled locks of hair from her brow.

It really was a superb room, she thought, as she gazed heavy-eyed at her surroundings. The ancient four-poster bed with its delicate, barley-sugar-twist posts was draped with swaths of pale blue embroidered silk damask, which matched the curtains hanging either side of the tall windows. The elegant gilt chairs, also covered in blue silk, were obviously every bit as old and rare as the Aubusson carpet, whose faded colours of deep pink, ivory and gold lent a warm, comforting glow to the bedroom.

However, despite being surrounded by such magnificence, Louisa couldn't remember a time when she had ever felt quite so lonely and unhappy. How was it that she — who had always prided herself on being *so* thoroughly sensible and down to earth—could have become involved in such an extraordinary and bizarre situation? In fact, having become so completely disorientated over the past few days, she'd even begun to wonder whether she was caught up in the midst of some terrible, frightening dream.

But although the scene downstairs, in Xavier's large sitting-room, had rapidly disintegrated into one of almost nightmare proportions, she couldn't escape the fact that she had, goodness knows how, become enmeshed in a disastrous scenario which was, alas, only too real.

When Xavier had dropped his bombshell, by announcing that he and Louisa must be married immediately, his words had been followed by a shocked, deafening silence. In the hushed lull—during which one could have easily heard a pin drop on to the thick Persian carpet—Louisa had stared at him in open-mouthed astonishment and disbelief. Quite certain, at first, that there must be something wrong with her hearing, she had rapidly begun to wonder if she wasn't also in danger of losing her mind. *Marriage. . .?* To *Xavier*—of all people! Oh, no. . .it simply wasn't possible. . . She *must* have completely misunderstood what he'd been saying.

But even as her tired brain had struggled to try to understand what was going on, she had nearly jumped out of her skin as Désirée had given a loud shriek of rage and fury. Dramatically throwing herself down on to a nearby sofa, she had produced several earth-shattering screams, before swiftly lapsing into a fit of raving hysterics.

Amid the ensuing uproar and pandemonium—the noise and confusion made even worse by Tante Sophie's loud cries and lamentations—it was impossible to even think clearly. Unfortunately, Marie-Thérèse's prompt action, in seizing hold of a large vase of flowers and swiftly emptying its contents down over Désirée's head, only made the situation ten times worse.

'*Look*!' Désirée screeched at Xavier. 'Just *look* what your niece has done to me!' Drumming her heels and yelling blue murder, she frantically tried to pull pieces of flowers, leaves and twigs from her hair, which had, only a few minutes before, been a charming arrangement of dark, glossy curls. But now, as she jerkily plucked the remaining bits of greenery and crushed petals from the thick mass of her wet and tangled coils, all sophistication and glamour appeared to have deserted the petite woman.

'I demand. . . I insist. . . I shall telephone my lawyers. . .the police. . .!' she screamed. Already almost incoherent with fury, her rage was further fuelled, if that were possible, by Marie-Thérèse's peals of cruel, mocking laughter.

Amid the noise and commotion, it was some moments before Louisa noticed that, of all the people in the room, Xavier seemed to be the only one totally unfazed by the fracas. Standing still, as though in the eye of a storm, he appeared completely relaxed, regarding the chaos and tumult eddying about his tall, silent figure with a lofty, aristorcratic expression of sardonic amusement.

However, with Marie-Thérèse and Désirée now locked in battle as they yelled loudly at one another, and Tante Sophie tearfully pleading for him to intervene, Xavier eventually gave a bored shrug of his shoulders, before proceeding to take a firm grip on the situation.

Louisa was surprised to note that he hardly needed to raise his voice to instantly command everyone's attention. Indeed, it seemed that within the twinkling of an eye he'd successfully calmed down his elderly aunt, addressed a few harsh words to his niece — which had the effect of reducing the young girl to a shame-faced silence — and, after refusing to allow Désirée to drive herself home, he was firmly escorting his still violently protesting girlfriend from the room.

'As for you, Louisa. . .' he said, pausing in the doorway to turn the searchlight beam of his dark, glittering eyes on her dazed and bewildered figure. 'I fully intend for you and I to have a long talk on my return.'

Louisa was almost sure that she'd caught a note of deep, sardonic amusement in Xavier's bland voice, before the door closed behind him. But, since there was nothing even *faintly* amusing about the situation, she realised that she must have been mistaken.

Left on their own, the three women stared at each other in silence for a few moments. Until, at last, Marie-Thérèse broke the increasingly tense atmosphere.

'What on earth is going on?' she frowned. 'Did my uncle actually say. . .? I mean, is he *really* intending to marry you?'

'No — of course he isn't,' Louisa mumbled, quickly bending down to pick up some of the wet leaves on the carpet. 'It was just a bad joke, that's all.'

'But he isn't the sort of man who makes jokes like that,' the girl persisted. 'What do you think, Tante?'

The older woman gave a heavy sigh. 'I no longer know *what* to think. However, while I do not care for Désirée, I must agree with my nephew: it was very wrong of you to throw that vase of flowers at her. Just look at the mess!' she grumbled, tugging the bell rope for Rosa to come and clear up the room. 'These sort of noisy, hysterical scenes are definitely not good for a woman of my age,' she added querulously, placing a trembling hand on her chest. 'I'm sure my doctor would agree. He always says that I have to be careful, and——'

Marie-Thérèse gave a snort of laughter. 'Come off it, Tante! You know that your doctor says you have the constitution of an ox! And besides,' she added, putting a comforting arm around the elderly woman's slight figure, 'just think what a wonderful time you'll have, making all the arrangements for the wedding.'

'For heaven's sake!' Louisa exclaimed nervously, her cheeks flaming as the two other women turned to stare at her. 'Why can't you both understand that there isn't going to be a wedding?'

'But my uncle said——'

'I don't care *what* he said!' she retorted firmly. 'As

far as *I'm* concerned, I have absolutely no intention of tripping down the aisle with Xavier — or anyone else!'

Tante Sophie, who had immediately perked up at the idea of having to organise a wedding, was now regarding the English girl with some interest.

'You're very tall, of course,' she murmured. 'So possibly an elegant, classical style of dress would suit you best. With maybe just a few flowers in your hair, and——'

'Forget it!' Louisa snapped grimly, ashamed to be speaking quite so rudely to a woman considerably older than herself, but anxious to make herself very clearly understood. 'I am definitely *not* going to marry your nephew. In fact, I'm only interested in driving away from this castle, as soon as possible.'

Marie-Thérèse gave her a puzzled frown. 'I thought you told me that your car had broken down?'

'Yes, I'm afraid it has,' Louisa sighed. 'But surely there must be some form of transport I can borrow to get back to my hotel in Ajaccio?'

The French girl shook her head. 'I can't help you, I'm afraid. You see, my uncle refuses to let me drive on the mountain roads — he says that they are far too dangerous. And, since Tante Sophie and I have been taken everywhere by my uncle's chauffeur, Franco, I have no idea what vehicles are in the garage.'

When appealed to, the elderly woman was equally uninformative. 'I do not concern myself with such matters,' she shrugged, before looking closely at the English girl, who was clearly swaying with fatigue. 'You seem very tired, my dear, and not in a fit state to drive a car. I really think that you ought to spend the night here with us.'

'Tante Sophie's quite right,' Marie-Thérèse chimed in. 'And then — if you feel you must go — we can maybe arrange some transport tomorrow morning,' she added as Rosa knocked and entered the room.

Feeling totally drained and exhausted, Louisa was simply too weary to argue the subject any further. After refusing the young girl's suggestion that they should relax with a strong drink before supper, she'd concentrated all her remaining energies on firmly requesting to be taken to a spare bedroom.

'But. . .but what will I say to my uncle, when he returns?' Marie-Thérèse had asked apprehensively while leading her from the room, clearly not looking forward to the return of her formidable guardian.

'I couldn't care less *what* you say to him,' Louisa muttered wearily as she stumbled up the first steps of the wide staircase. 'I'm only interested in a good night's sleep!'

But now, with the hours and minutes ticking slowly by in the small hours of the night, Louisa realised that it had been a forlorn hope. Although exactly why she should be still feeling so tense and unable to relax, she had no idea.

It was true that living a relatively quiet life in London, and concentrating on her job—almost to the extent of becoming a workaholic—she wasn't used to a rumbustious family life. Indeed, she'd never before experienced such a torrent of shattering noise and dramatic histrionics as that produced by Désirée tonight. So maybe that was why she was still feeling so upset and disturbed by the completely unexpected, traumatic scene in Xavier's sitting-room, why the blessed relief of sleep continued to evade her.

But it was no good trying to fool herself, Louisa thought miserably. In reality, it was Xavier's statement that he intended to marry her which was dominating her mind to the exclusion of all else. Quite apart from anything else, she bitterly resented being used as some kind of pawn by Xavier. If he wanted to play such foolish, complicated games with his relations it still didn't give him any right to drag *her* into a family quarrel. And why he should have gone completely over the top, she had no idea.

It was impossible to believe that Xavier was seriously proposing marriage—simply because he'd been discovered making love to her. After all, such an attractive man must have made love to *hundreds* of women, she reminded herself, dismally aware of the fact that she was only the latest in a long, long line of such conquests. So her original conclusion — that it must be a very bad joke on his part — was probably correct.

Unfortunately, despite all the stern logic and sense, which she'd been desperately trying to summon to her aid over the past few hours, Louisa was finding it impossible to rid her mind and tembling body of the devastating effect of Xavier's powerful embrace. Even now, she could almost tangibly feel the hard strength of his arms about her, the burning, passionate desire which had scorched through her trembling limbs beneath the powerful effect of his kisses. . .

With a sob, Louisa turned to bury her face in the pillows, trying to shut her mind and body to the throbbing ache in the pit of her stomach, the shameful recollection of how she'd moaned with pleasure at the mastery of his touch.

Eventually slipping into a disturbed and fitful sleep, Louisa woke up the next morning still feeling tired and sluggish. It seemed as though the whole world were pressing hard down on her still weary figure, her depression deepening as she realised that she had little or no chance of leaving the castle — not without yet another confrontation with Xavier.

Not even the arrival of a young maid, bearing a tray of delicious croissants and freshly brewed coffee, could help to lift her spirits. If only she were in better physical shape, she might be able to cope with this strange, foreign household and the depth of her feelings for Xavier. But even having a shower in the luxurious *en-suite* bathroom didn't seem to make much difference to her almost dizzy feeling of displacement — as though her legs were made of jelly, and her head stuffed full of cotton wool.

However, after putting on the fresh blouse and skirt which Marie-Thérèse had given her late last night, she eventually summoned up enough courage to force herself to leave the room. Trailing slowly and reluctantly down the wide oak staircase, she wasn't sure whether to be relieved or not on discovering that Xavier wasn't in his sitting-room. With no visible sign of any of the other members of the family, she wandered slowly and dejectedly through one empty, magnificent room after another. It wasn't until she was passing an open doorway, and she heard her name being called, that she realised she wasn't alone in the huge old castle.

'Good morning, Louisa!'

With a sudden lurch in her stomach at the sound of that unmistakeable dark, husky voice, Louisa slowly turned, reluctantly retracing her steps to enter a large, baronial-sized dining-room.

'I trust you slept well?' Xavier enquired coolly, from where he sat at the end of a long, heavily carved oak table, which looked every bit as ancient as the castle. 'Have you had breakfast?'

'No, I. . .I wasn't hungry,' she muttered, still hovering uncertainly in the doorway.

'It is foolish not to eat something,' he told her sternly, putting down his copy of the *Corse Matin* newspaper. Rising to his feet, he pulled out a chair at the table beside him.

Louisa shook her head. 'I really don't feel like——'

'Come and sit down,' he commanded in a steely tone of voice.

She hesitated for a moment, but after a swift glance at his hard and determined expression she realised that it was pointless to protest any further.

After pouring her some fresh coffee from the large silver pot on the table and passing her a plate piled high with fresh, warm croissants and brioches, he returned to his seat.

'You must try to eat something,' Xavier told her firmly. As she hesitated, he smiled. 'Come, Louisa, you must taste our locally made honey. I can assure you that it is delicious!'

Helplessly bemused by his unexpected smile, which made her feel suddenly breathless and dizzy, she tentatively did as she was told.

'That's better. I understand that you did not eat any dinner last night. It cannot do you any good to go without food for such a long time.'

Surprised by the warm, concerned note in his voice, Louisa stole a quick sideways glance at Xavier's tall figure, dressed casually in tan trousers, his open-necked black shirt seeming to fit his wide shoulders like a glove, while the short sleeves displayed his muscular arms.

She flushed, a tight knot suddenly clenching in the pit of her stomach as she quickly averted her eyes from the figure radiating such a powerful aura of strong, virile masculinity.

'Er—talking about last night. . .' She hesitated, wondering how on earth she could even begin to broach the subject. After all, it wasn't just she who'd been left in a fog of confusion. Even Tante Sophie and Marie-Thérèse hadn't been entirely sure what Xavier had meant. Which prompted her to ask, 'Have your aunt and Marie-Thérèse already had breakfast?'

'Yes. Tante Sophie has taken my niece to an art and music festival, which one of her friends is helping to organise at Oletta—a pretty village which lies north of here, on the east coast. I thought you would be interested to hear some of our traditional Corsican folk music, and so we will be joining my aunt and Marie-Thérèse later on today.'

'Oh, no. . . I'm, sorry—but I'm afraid that I must return to Ajaccio,' she told him hurriedly, trying to steady her trembling hands. 'I am, of course, very— um—very grateful to you for allowing me to stay the night. But I really must get back to my hotel, as soon as possible.'

Xavier gave a brief shake of his dark head. 'I can see no point in your doing so.'

'All the same,' she muttered nervously, 'I really must insist on going back to Ajaccio. I have several arrange-ments to make, and——'

'Your future arrangements are now *my* concern,' he drawled, casually pouring himself another cup of dark coffee. 'I have informed the manager of your hotel that from now on you will be staying with my family, up here at the castle.'

'You. . .you can't *do* that!' she protested angrily.

'Really?' He lifted a dark, sardonic eyebrow. 'Nevertheless, my dear Louisa, I think you will find that I already have!'

'But. . .but what about all my clothes. . .my luggage? And I haven't even paid the hotel bill, for heaven's sake.'

Xavier shrugged his broad shoulders. 'There is no need for you to sound so distraught. Your account at the hotel has been settled, and all your luggage has already been brought back up here, to the castle. So, you see, there are no problems for you to worry about.'

'I can see that my problems are only just beginning!' she retorted angrily. 'You have absolutely *no* right to interfere in my life in this way!'

'I have every right,' he informed her smoothly. 'Since you are my future wife, it is only right and proper that you should be under the close chaperonage of my aunt. And since we are to be married in a few days' time — I'm sure you must see that it is merely a sensible arrangement.'

'*I don't believe it*! This *can't* be happening to me!' she wailed, burying her face in her hands for a moment as she struggled to pull her shattered wits together. 'I thought you were only joking last night. . .that you couldn't be serious. I mean, the whole idea is completely *mad*!' Louisa added fiercely, rallying her depleted forces as she glared at the handsome man. 'And *don't* waste your breath on any more nonsense about your "honour" — because I think the whole concept is totally ridiculous!'

Xavier gave a typically Gallic shrug of his shoulders. 'Nevertheless, it's the only course open to someone, such as myself, who believes in and reveres the traditions of their homeland.'

'But it means nothing to *me*!' she stormed. And then quickly realising that she wasn't going to get anywhere by yelling at him, she tried to force herself to calm down. Taking a deep, unsteady breath, she tried again.

'Please, Xavier — *please* try to see that what you're suggesting just doesn't make sense. For one thing, you know very little about me. And for another: even if I agreed to marry you—and there's *no way* that I am willing to do so—it would be nothing more than a marriage of convenience. I'm quite sure neither of us would want that,' she added desperately as he continued to regard her with an impassive, bland expression on his face.

'*Au contraire*, my dear Louisa. I see nothing wrong in a *mariage de convenance*. And neither, by your own admission, do you. After all,' he added as she opened her mouth to protest, 'that is exactly the sort of marriage which you were planning with your boyfriend in London, *non*?'

'No, that's not true!'

'But yes—that is *precisely* how you described your future plans,' he continued ruthlessly. 'You were quite clearly intending—at some future date—to marry your colleague, a remarkably foolish-sounding man who, by your own admission, does not even consider you to be a beautiful, attractive woman.' He shrugged. 'It was immediately obvious to me that you were in danger of making a grave mistake—and quite clearly not acting in your own best interests.'

'Why don't you mind your own business?' she muttered, her face flaming with embarrassment.

'You *are* my business!' Xavier gave her a sardonic smile, before continuing remorselessly, 'Let us consider the situation. This very boring young man, Neville, is neither wealthy nor the managing director of his firm. Nor does he appear to be at all concerned with your comfort and safety. For instance, I would *never* have agreed to allow my future wife to travel unescorted about Europe.' He looked at her sternly.

'Therefore, your choice of this man was not a sensible decision. Particularly, not for a girl who has no dowry, and who presents herself as an experienced, sophisticated woman of the world.'

'Well, I—er—that's not exactly how I see myself,' she murmured, staring at him in bemusement as she strove to try to keep some hold on reality. A dowry? What on earth was he talking about?

'But that is *precisely* how you present yourself, my

dear Louisa,' he pointed out smoothly. 'To be travelling on your own, and conducting business for a firm which trades in such a male-orientated field, it would naturally be assumed that you have considerable worldly experience of men.'

Louisa gazed at him in astonishment. Was he *really* saying that she appeared to be some sort of scarlet woman? If so, maybe Xavier should spend some time with her on a building site. Anywhere more unromantic would be hard to find!

He raised a dark eyebrow. 'You find what I have said amusing?'

'Yes. . .no. . . I mean, I'm afraid that you've got *completely* the wrong idea about me!'

'Really?' he drawled blandly, his lips twisted in a sardonic smile. 'I do not think so.'

'Oh, well—that's it. You know it all, right?' She glared at him in baffled fury.

'I know that I am a much better *parti*—a far more suitable match for you than your colleague, Neville,' he informed her bluntly. 'I am, after all, an exceedingly wealthy man. And, unlike your English boyfriend, I do know how to cherish and value a beautiful woman.'

'I just bet you do!' she muttered grimly, a shaft of green jealousy piercing her heart at the thought of all the other women who must have been attracted to him like metal filings to a magnet.

'But of course!' He gave her a wolfish, sexy grin which almost took her breath away. 'At thirty-five years of age, it would be very strange if I did not have *some* experience of women, would it not?'

'Yes, I suppose so. . .' she mumbled, her cheeks flushing as she stared fixedly down at the nervously twisting hands in her lap. 'But I still don't see why— er—well, I'm sorry to put it so crudely. . .but I can't see what's in it for you.'

Louisa raised her head, forcing herself to look him straight in the eye. 'Leaving aside all this "honour" business, why on earth should you want to marry me? Surely Désirée would be a far better proposition?

Especially since the woman's obviously mad about you,' she added waspishly.

He rose from the table, walking slowly over to gaze out of one of the large Gothic windows at the mountains in the distance. Even with his back to her, Xavier's tall figure seemed to exude a powerful aura, easily dominating the large room. She could feel her mouth suddenly becoming dry with tension—her quivering figure seized by a totally insane, crazy longing to be tightly clasped within those strong, muscular arms. I've got to get out of here! she told herself wildly, her hands becoming damp and clammy as she struggled to control the ultimately fatal, disastrous effect of his dark attraction on her weak, trembling body.

Totally immersed in her own dismal thoughts, Lousia did not realise for some moments that she must have missed part of what Xavier was saying. However, it soon became clear that he was anxious to avoid any further connection with Désirée, despite the heavy pressure exerted by her father, a neighbouring landowner. As Xavier informed her arrogantly, marriage to a woman who had been deserted by her husband—and who was given to melodramatic tantrums—was definitely not something he was willing to contemplate.

'Besides,' he added, turning to walk slowly towards Louisa, 'it is time I settled down and produced a family.'

'A f-family. . ?' Louisa gasped, staring up at him with dazed eyes.

'But of course. What could be more natural than wanting a son to carry on my name?'

Marriage. . .? A baby. . .? This couldn't be happening to her! Louisa told herself hysterically, frantically trying to stem the almost overriding tide of panic and alarm which was sweeping through her trembling figure. If, at any point, Xavier had indicated that he loved her—or, at the very least, cared deeply about her—her response might possibly have been very different. But the thought of entering such a cold-blooded contract, with a man who clearly only wished to rid himself of an over-eager mistress—while also gaining the added bonus of a son and heir was *totally* unacceptable.

'I. . .I'm not prepared to listen to any more of this nonsense!' she cried, jumping quickly to her feet. 'What you are suggesting is just the most. . .the most awful thing I've ever heard!'

Xavier gave a bark of deeply cynical laughter. 'Can it truly be such an "awful" fate — to marry a seriously rich man?' he drawled sardonically, quickly catching hold of her arm as she turned to flee the room. 'Would it *really* be so dreadful to be a countess, and to live surrounded by comfort and luxury for the rest of your days, to wear couture dresses and to be showered with jewels — or anything else which your heart may desire?'

Your love is the only thing which my heart desires! she wanted to scream at him as he drew her closer to his tall, commanding figure.

'You simply don't understand. . .' she wailed helplessly, desperately trying to resist the dark, enticing seduction of his overwhelming attraction. 'I don't *care* about money, or jewels — or any of the other items which you seem to think are so important. Can't you understand. . .?' she pleaded frantically. 'Can't you see that they are only material possessions — that they can mean *nothing*, if the two people concerned don't love each other?'

For one long moment Xavier's tall figure became still and rigid. As he stared intently down at the girl clasped in his arms, it seemed as though he was prepared to acknowledge the truth of what she said. And then a strange, almost painful expression seemed to flicker briefly across his face, before he gave a careless shrug of his broad shoulders.

'You are, of course, quite right. Love is very important,' he agreed slowly. 'But — who can say? — such feelings may very well grow in time, *non*? In the meantime, my dear Louisa,' he murmured, his voice thickening as he drew her soft, trembling figure against his hard body, 'there can be no denying that we are both deeply attracted to one another, hmm?'

'But that's merely lust!' she protested helplessly as the iron grip of his arms tightened about her.

'It is enough for me, at the moment,' he murmured huskily as his dark head came down towards her, and he slowly trailed his lips over her forehead to her temple, and on down her cheek.

But not enough for *me*! she thought despairingly, completely unable to control the rising tide of desire which coursed through her quivering body; nor could she prevent a low moan as his mouth finally touched a corner of her lips.

Slowly and tantalisingly, Xavier explored her soft, trembling mouth with small, seductive kisses, before his warm, firm lips gradually became more insistent. Louisa felt as though she were drowning, helplessly swept along on a dark tide of erotic excitement, his kiss deepening as he forced her lips apart, sensuously exploring the inner softness of her mouth in an erotic invasion of her stunned senses.

With her emotions spinning wildly out of control, she felt as though she were falling down into a deep abyss, the burning pressure of his mouth, and the hard force of the body pressed so closely to her own, igniting an irresistible flame within her. Her entire being seemed to be dissolving in a molten heap of desire and excitement—totally seduced by a deep hunger that matched his own—as his lovemaking became more roughly sensual and demanding.

She was totally lost. This was all she had ever wanted out of life—the very pinnacle of all her half-formed, uncertain romantic dreams of sensual love and fulfilment.

Xavier slowly and reluctantly raised his dark head, staring down at the girl who now lay like a limp rag doll in his arms. Gazing at her swollen lips, and the green eyes dazed with languorous desire, he gave a short bark of triumphant laughter.

'So—we will be married, yes?'

'Yes. . .' she whispered helplessly, her legs feeling as though they were made of cotton wool as Xavier led her trembling, unresisting figure from the room.

CHAPTER NINE

LOUISA glanced down at the large ring on her finger. The heart-shaped ruby surrounded by huge diamonds flashed in the shafts of brilliant sunlight streaming in through the windows of the chauffeured limousine. Over the past few days she had become used to wearing the enormously expensive ring. However, it was the slim gold band, now also firmly clasping the fourth finger of her left hand, which caused her to give a deep sigh of complete incomprehension.

Louisa turned her head to gaze blindly out of the window. On leaving the town hall, she had barely noticed the shops and cafés in the Cours Paoli. And even now, as the vehicle made its way back through the steep, winding streets of the ancient town of Corte, perched on a rocky outcrop above a deep ravine, she still wasn't in a fit state to appreciate the beauty and grandeur of the scenery which lay beyond the bridge, over the swiftly flowing Tavignano river. As they swept along the narrow, twisting route that carved its way through the rocky gorges of the Restonica valley, leading back to Xavier's castle in the mountains, she felt like pinching herself—just to make sure that she was awake. It seemed almost impossible to believe that she really *had* just taken part in a civil marriage ceremony, and was now sitting next to her new husband—Xavier d'Erlanger, Comte Cinarchesi.

Her *husband*! How could she have married a man whom she'd met only two weeks ago? A man about whom she knew virtually nothing? Apart from the quite inexplicable fact that she loved him, Louisa quickly reminded herself. It was all she'd had to cling to during these past few days. Totally bemused and bewildered, it was as though she'd been existing in a hazy trance—moving, like a wooden puppet, to the strings so firmly manipulated by Xavier.

Turning her head to cast a swift glance at his dark, handsome profile, Louisa could still hardly believe that this was happening to her, that she'd allowed herself to be steamrollered into submission by Xavier's deliberate use of his undoubted physical attraction. And she still didn't believe that his actions had been dictated solely by his sense of personal honour.

Back in England, such a statement would be guaranteed to produce raised eyebrows, if not gales of sophisticated hilarity and mirth. And that had, of course, been her own initial reaction to Xavier's words. But, although she'd only been on this unspoilt and yet somehow mysterious island for such a short time, Louisa was beginning to realise that there were two sides to Corsica. Hidden just beneath the surface of its tourist image, and the modern-day veneer as a *departement* of France, lay a completely unique and darkly traditional way of life.

Nothing could have illustrated this better than her visit to the festival at Oletta.

Still feeling totally shattered from her forced agreement to marry Xavier, in the dining-room of the castle earlier that morning, Louisa had completely forgotten about Tante Sophie's involvement with the festival. However, by the time she found herself in Xavier's fast sports car, with the vehicle speeding along the dangerous mountain roads, she was so paralysed with mental exhaustion that she neither knew nor cared *where* he was taking her. It wasn't until they were leaving the mountains behind them that she began to appreciate the sheer beauty of her surroundings. Through the hazy mist clouding her mind, she realised that the foothills were covered with acres of wild flowers, whose colours of pale-blue, white and deep purple sparkled in the sunlight, like an enormous Persian carpet which had been rolled out for her delight. And, once again, she became conscious of the intoxicating, spicy scent of the *maquis* — for which, as Xavier pointed out, Corsica was justly famous.

When they stopped at a roadside tavern, eating a light meal at tables set outside under the chestnut trees,

the heady perfume of the aromatic shrub seemed
almost overpowering. So much so that, although
Xavier maintained a flow of polite conversation, she
could only offer disjointed murmurs in reply—the
narcotic aroma producing a giddy, light-headed effect
on her already dazed senses. By the time they eventually reached Oletta, she felt as though she'd completely
lost touch with reality, drifting dreamily like a sleep-
walker, as they left the car to join the crowds winding
their way through the main street of the village.

The setting sun threw a deep red glow on the old
stone houses, nestling amid groves of chestnut trees on
the hillside, from which could be seen a distant view of
the sea. It was a charming scene, with the inhabitants,
young and old, enthusiastically welcoming the many
car-loads of happy, laughing visitors, as they joined the
cheerful, jostling crowd already filling the village
square.

'Why is everyone arriving so late in the day?' Louisa
asked, gazing with bewilderment at the mass of people
eddying past them. 'Surely the festival must be over by
now?'

'Many events have already taken place, of course,'
Xavier agreed, putting a protective arm about her as
he steered her slim figure towards a café on the other
side of the square. 'However, there is a very special
event this evening—a concert of our traditional
Corsican folk-songs, which I particularly wanted you to
hear.'

Obviously the sort of man to instantly command the
attention of waiters, Xavier seemed to have no difficulty in gaining hold of some vacant chairs. And when
they were joined by his aunt, Louisa's dizzy and
confused state of mind enabled her to numbly accept
what might have been an embarrassing encounter.
Because Xavier—clearly determined to cut the ground
from beneath her—had already, it seemed, informed
his aunt of his future plans.

'Ah, there you are—at last!' Tante Sophie
exclaimed, leaning over to plant an enthusiastic kiss on
the younger girl's pale cheek. 'I'm so *thrilled* to hear

the news. I'm sure you'll both be very happy. And you can just leave everything to me!' she added gaily as Louisa gave her a vague, bemused smile. 'I'm going to have a wonderful time making all the arrangements, so you'll have no need to worry your pretty head about such matters.'

Louisa wasn't sure whether Xavier deliberately changed the subject to spare her blushes, but his query regarding the success of the festival managed to deflect Tante Sophie's clearly obsessive interest in the subject of his imminent marriage.

'Oh, yes—it's all been *such* a success!' his aunt told him enthusiastically. 'As you know, the main festival is normally held here in August. But it's become so popular that the committee decided to have a small, extra event this spring. And you really should have listened to the folk group from Peru—they were *formidable*!'

'Well, you seem to be enjoying yourself, Tante!' Xavier laughed, before adding, 'But I don't see Marie-Thérèse anywhere.'

'No.' His aunt shook her head. 'She's joined up with some friends, whom she met a few summers ago, and she'll be joining us later. They are perfectly respectable,' she added quickly as his brow creased in a frown. 'And I must tell you, Xavier, that now you are getting married—and about time too!—you ought to allow her more freedom. After all, your niece is now a young woman—and well able to look after herself.'

Bravo, Tante! Louisa thought, silently cheering on the frail, bird-like figure of the elderly woman, who was so surprisingly standing up to her fierce nephew.

But even more surprising was the fact that Xavier merely gave a nonchalant shrug of his shoulders. 'You may be right,' he murmured, before the crowd erupted into noisy cheers and whistles as a group of musicians entered the square.

Although she'd never attended a folk concert before, Louisa found that she was enjoying herself. However, she remained somewhat puzzled by Xavier's remark earlier. While the performers were obviously very

good, she couldn't honestly feel that any of them had
been particularly outstanding. However, in her present
confused and muddled state of mind, she was grateful
for the soothing balm of the music on her battered
senses.

As darkness fell and a cool, chilly breeze eddied
about the village square, Louisa was touched when
Xavier, who'd left his seat some moments before,
returned with a soft woollen car rug, which he placed
carefully about her shoulders. She was just turning to
thank him for his unexpectedly kind gesture when a
hush fell over the audience. Peering through the spot-
light trained on to the small stage, Louisa saw that it
was now occupied by a plump, rather plain and dowdy-
looking figure. Dressed all in black, the woman stood
absolutely still for a few moments, the silent crowd
almost seeming to hold its breath, before she began to
sing without any musical accompaniment.

'She is singing a *voceru*,' Xavier whispered in Louisa's
ear, explaining that it was an authentically traditional
song, freely improvised in the old Corsican language —
in this case, a lament for the death of a favourite
child.

The overwhelming grief, so plainly evident in the
song, left Louisa feeling stunned and shaken. Slivers of
ice seemed to be shivering down her back, the anguish
in the high-pitched voice so bare and naked that she
felt as though she were being pierced to the heart.

As the final notes of the music shivered on the still
air, the crowd remained silent for some moments,
before their thunderous applause filled the dark square.
Many in the crowd were weeping openly, and Louisa
was herself unable to prevent tears from welling up in
her eyes, and slowly trickling down her cheek.

She understood, at last, why Xavier had brought her
all the way to Oletta. The woman's deeply melancholic
voice had wrenched away the mask of everyday modern
life. For a brief period of time, both the singer and her
listeners had been transported back to the old Corsican
traditions, when such female lamentations, mourning
the dead and demanding justice, accompanied the

brutal acts of the vendetta. And it was, as Xavier must have intended, a soul-stirring and harshly poignant reminder of the dark, sombre emotions which lay submerged beneath the present-day, apparently sophisticated veneer of the island.

'I, too, never fail to be moved by such a song,' Tante Sophie murmured, brushing her eyes with a lace handkerchief before preparing to rejoin her friends, with whom she was due to spend the night.

'I will send Franco to bring you home tomorrow,' Xavier told the elderly woman, and then slowly led Louisa's tired figure back to where he had parked the car.

'That song was so. . .so heartbreaking,' she murmured, when they were once more on the road leading south.

'The *voceru* is a very ancient tradition, and part of our culture which almost died without trace,' he said. 'Fortunately, there has recently been a considerable revival of our ancient customs. Perhaps one day—if you're very lucky—you may have the opportunity to hear the *paghiella*. Sung by men, it is a primitive and war-like incantation, whose origins are lost in the midst of time. Unfortunately,' he added with a slight shrug, 'it is very rarely heard nowadays.'

For a long time, leaning back in her seat with her eyes closed, Louisa imagined that she could still hear the plaintive notes of the melancholic lament, which so accurately reflected her own heavy depression. She knew that it would remain with her, as a lasting impression of a quite extraordinary day.

It was also a day in which Xavier—that most arrogant of men—had shown that he could also be kind and sympathetic. It was this unexpected side of him which gave her the courage to raise a particularly awkward subject.

'What—er—what are you planning to do about my stepbrother? Are you still insisting on his marriage to Marie-Thérèse?'

There was a long silence in the car as he skilfully

navigated a hairpin bend. 'No,' he said at last. 'No — I have decided not to pursue that particular matter.'

Louisa's initial feeling of considerable relief gradually gave way to puzzlement. 'Why not?' she asked, turning to gaze at his stern profile, thrown into sharp relief as a shaft of moonlight pierced the shadowy darkness within the car. 'I mean. . .it isn't that I'm not pleased you've given up the idea. But I can't help wondering why you've changed your mind.'

He gave a short bark of rueful laughter. 'Really, my dear Louisa,' he drawled. 'Don't you think that *one* marriage between our two families is quite enough?'

'Yes, well — you're quite right,' she agreed. 'But I don't see why you should still be insisting on *our* marriage. After all, there doesn't seem to be any difference, and——'

'The two cases are quite different,' he retorted. But, when she pressed him once again on the point, he resolutely refused to discuss the matter any further.

Yawning with weariness and exhaustion after such a traumatic day, she decided to drop the subject — for the moment. Her senses lulled by the rhythmic, purring drone of the car's powerful engine, Louisa's last conscious thoughts were that since she had — one way or another — saved Jamie from disaster, she ought to be able to do the same for herself. After all, it shouldn't be too difficult to find some form of transport, no matter how ancient, which would enable her to reach the airport at Ajaccio, and catch a plane to England.

Having slept for the rest of the journey back to the castle, she had fallen dog-tired on to the bed in the guest room, not waking until after eleven o'clock the next morning. After such a long sleep, she was feeling in a far more refreshed and relaxed state of mind. Full of plans to avoid the marriage upon which Xavier seemed so determined, it was some time before she could bring herself to realise that he had — with considerable guile and cunning — completely spiked her guns.

Although she was once again in possession of her handbag, the search for which had originally brought

her to the castle, it didn't take her very long to realise
that her passport was missing. And when she chal-
lenged Xavier as to its whereabouts she nearly
exploded with rage when he blandly informed her that
he was arranging for it to be renewed, in her new
married name.

'I can see no reason for you to need it *before* our
marriage,' he drawled blandly. But the sardonic amusement in his dark, gleaming eyes only fuelled her anger
and outrage at his action.

'That's a *British* passport!' she informed him through
clenched teeth. 'You had no right to take it without my
permission!'

Xavier gave a deep rumble of cynical laughter. 'I
thought it was we French who were supposed to be so
nationalistic? It would seem that we can hardly hold a
candle to the British!'

'I want it back—right away!' she insisted stubbornly.

'I can assure you that there's no need to make such
a fool of yourself, Louisa!' he drawled, with an arrogance which she found absolutely *maddening*. 'I have
merely arranged for it to be taken to the nearest British
consulate, for renewal. And, in any case,' he added
crushingly, 'not only do you become a Frenchwoman
on our marriage, but, as you must surely know, it is
only a matter of time before all EC countries will have
the same documentation. So let us hear no more of this
trivial matter, hmm?'

There was absolutely nothing she could do, Louisa
told herself, suddenly quite certain that it wasn't love
which she felt for this man, but pure unadulterated
hatred! Rigid with fury, she glared at Xavier, whose
lips were twitching with barely suppressed, silent laughter. Despite knowing that he was deliberately keeping
the passport well out of her way until their marrige,
she couldn't prove that he was acting in anything but
her best interests. And without that document there
was no way she could escape from the island.

The bustling arrival of Tante Sophie momentarily
lifted her gloomy spirits. But after having to put up
with the elderly woman's misty-eyed, romantic view of

the forthcoming nuptials, and her frantic preparations for the wedding, Louisa found herself growing heartily sick of the whole subject. Proceeding to go completely over the top, Tante Sophie never seemed to be off the telephone, arranging visits from the dressmaker, the florist, the caterers and goodness knows who else, while making constant references to what she called, 'the happy day!' Fond though she had become of the older woman, Louisa found that there were several times when she had to dash out of the room before she gave in to an almost overwhelming compulsion to murder the elderly lady.

The only item on which Louisa was *not* prepared to compromise was the matter of her wedding-dress. Practically breaking Tante Sophie's heart, she resolutely refused to have any of the frills and flounces on which Xavier's aunt had set her heart. Luckily, she found an ally in the dressmaker. Prepared to make a short wedding dress in only a few days, the woman — whose mouth always seemed to be full of dangerous-looking pins — enthusiastically agreed with Louisa's own choice, of a classically plain and simple dress in heavy cream silk.

It was when she was having a final fitting of the dress, with Tante Sophie shaking her head in despair at the lack of any ornate embroidery or decoration to relieve the severe style, that the elderly woman raised the question of Xavier's first wife.

Quite why Louisa hadn't given any thought to her beautiful predecessor, she had no idea. Of course, in all the hurried arrangements over the past few days, there were times when she was barely able to remember her own name! but with Tante Sophie extolling the virtues of 'dear Georgette' — who'd apparently gone to *her* wedding in a ravishing display of satin and lace strewn with diamanté, courtesy of the House of Dior — Louisa suddenly realised that she now had an additional burden and cause for alarm.

Although Xavier's first wife had been dead for some years, her lovely memory still seemed to be alive and well in Tante Sophie's mind. Even Marie-Thérèse, although she'd only been a young girl at the time, was still able to remember Georgette's outstanding beauty. So, with Xavier almost bound to be remembering and recalling the happy days of his first marriage, how could she possibly hope to compete or compare with such a paragon? Especially since the passage of time could only have enhanced the memory of Georgette's lovely face and figure. It was a deeply depressing state of affairs, which gave Louisa many tortuous and sleepless nights.

In fact, with so many problems crowding her weary brain, and the additional nagging worry of Xavier's feelings about his first wife, she was sure that she would have gone completely out of her mind, if it hadn't been for Rosa and Marie-Thérèse.

The plump housekeeper, who'd clearly indicated her delight at her master's choice of bride, had been a calm and stabilising influence in the hectic, frenzied atmosphere of the old castle. And with Xavier absent for some days, on a sudden business trip to Paris, Louisa and his niece had been given the opportunity to get to know each other, and to become firm friends.

Although Marie-Thérèse was clearly pleased about her uncle's forthcoming marriage, she was undoubtedly more perceptive than his aunt.

'I'm obviously pleased to know that Uncle Xavier has dropped his insane, crazy idea of my marrying your stepbrother,' she told Louisa with a heartfelt sigh of relief. 'But what about you? Is this wedding in a few day's time, what you *really* want? Are you truly happy?'

Louisa, who couldn't think how to explain all the ramifications of her forthcoming marriage to Xavier — and certainly not her present love-hate feelings for the man — had merely replied that yes, of course she was happy. But Marie-Thérèse had possibly caught the nervous, panic-stricken note behind her bland words, because she occasionally found the young girl regarding her with a questioning, puzzled expression on her face.

Despite seeming to agree with all the arrangements for her wedding — and with Xavier still conspicuous by his absence in Paris—Louisa had been determined to find some route of escape. And it was with this aim in mind that she'd telephoned both Jamie and Neville Frost. While she had little hope of her stepbrother proving to be anything more than a broken reed, she did have high hopes of receiving some concrete assistance from Neville.

As she'd suspected, her call to Jamie was more or less a waste of time. He wasn't at all surprised to hear there was no need to worry about the loss of either his job or his fiancée. 'I *knew* that you'd manage to sort it out for me, Lou,' he told her cheerfully, before adding that he and Sonia were very happy, busy making preparations for their wedding in July.

Depressed by Jamie's blithe, selfish attitude, she couldn't bring herself to tell him that she was going to marry Marie-Thérèse's 'wicked uncle'. There seemed no point in doing so, especially when he was so full of his own news that he hadn't bothered to ask when she was returning to England.

When Louisa rang Neville, she knew that it might be embarrassing to have to confess her entanglement with Xavier. But she was sure her colleague's clever, agile brain would be able to think of a way for her to wriggle out of the mess in which she found herself. However, by the end of the call, Louisa knew that she had reached one of the lowest points of her existence.

Neville had been delighted to hear from her. 'Clever girl! You've certainly made the right choice in Xavier d'Erlanger—but then, I always knew that you'd land on your feet!' he chortled, giving her no chance to ask how he'd heard about her forthcoming marriage. However, she was astounded when Neville expressed his deep gratitude to Xavier, who, it appeared, had just bought a controlling share in the firm.

'Terrifically clever chap—really brilliant, in fact. Even *I* didn't know our firm was in financial hot water, mainly over investments in the new Docklands,' Neville explained. 'Before anyone knows what's hit them, Monsieur d'Erlanger has jetted into London, cleared out the dead wood by sacking most of the old partners, and *then*. . .you'll never believe it, Lou—but he's made *me* the new managing director! How about *that*?'

Louisa could hardly bear to listen as Neville—pleased as punch, and full of the joys of spring, tra-la!—had expounded his many ideas for revitalising the firm.

So much for Neville—yet another broken reed! she thought, feeling almost sick with frustration and anger as she slammed down the telephone. But he had, of course, been quite right; Xavier *was* very clever. He'd effectively bought off Neville—the only person who might have been able to help her—and had left her powerless to do anything, other than numbly accept her fate.

Xavier's return yesterday, only twenty-four hours before their wedding, had done little to help matters. With an almost continuous headache, her brain throbbing and pounding as she acknowledged the masterly precision which he'd used to cut off all her lines of retreat, she hadn't even had the satisfaction of quarrelling with the man.

On the few occasions when she had found herself alone with him, Xavier had given her no opportunity either to discuss his acquisition of the London firm or begin any conversation about their marriage, which was clearly doomed to disaster. Every time she'd tried to raise either subject, his only answer had been to clasp her tightly in his arms, before kissing her so soundly that all sense had been completely driven from her dazed and bemused mind.

In fact it wasn't until he'd joined her in the limousine, as they'd left for the town hall in Corte, earlier this morning, that she'd had any opportunity for a private conversation.

But by then, of course, it was far too late. Maybe she could have run away—but where to? And, even if she had managed to escape, she was certain that Xavier would somehow have discovered where she'd gone.

But that wasn't her chief worry at the moment. As much as she'd tried not to think about it, she still didn't know how she was going to cope with Xavier when

they were finally left alone together. He seemed to
have assumed that she was an experienced woman of
the world—whereas, in reality, she'd had practically
no 'experience' at all. Unfortunately, her only brief
experiment with sex, some years ago, had proved to be
an unmitigated disaster. And now, not only was she
afraid that Xavier would find her boringly gauche and
ignorant, but she knew that she hadn't a hope of being
favourably compared with his first wife, the beautiful
and lovely Georgette.

To marry such a breathtakingly handsome man, who
could obviously take his pick from any number of
attractive and sexy women, would have been a risky
business at the best of times. And whereas she had
subconsciously hoped that he might, in some miraculous fashion, eventually be able to return her love, it
really was about time she faced the hard facts of life.
While it was true that they were attracted to one
another, she was rapidly beginning to realise that
simply wasn't enough—certainly not enough on which
to base a marriage. The likelihood of his coming to
love her as she loved him now seemed so remote as to
be virtually impossible. And now that she was also
worried sick about making an utter fool of herself in
bed, it was all she could do not to burst into tears.

'Not long now.'

'Mmm. . .?' Louisa gave a start, blinking nervously
at her new husband as she realised that she'd been so
sunk in her own, deeply depressing thoughts that she
hadn't heard what he'd been saying.

'There is no need to look so worried,' Xavier murmured, placing a surprisingly warm and comforting
hand over her nervous, trembling fingers. 'I was merely
saying that we will soon be back at the castle.'

Gazing at the pale, wan figure of his new bride, who
was nevertheless looking very beautiful in the short,
straight dress of cream silk, whose classical design
acted as a foil to the brilliant colour of her shoulder-
length, red-gold hair, he added softly, 'Relax, Louisa!
There is no need to worry. A wedding reception—even
one organised by Tante Sophie—cannot last forever!'

'Yes, I know. That's exactly what I'm afraid of,' she retorted quickly, before suddenly flushing to the roots of her hair as she realised just how she had betrayed her innermost worries.

'I promise you—there is no need to fear me,' he murmured softly. 'So, please, *chérie*—do try not to look as though you are facing the guillotine!'

That sounds like a fairly accurate description of how I feel, she thought grimly, saved from having to reply as the limousine drew up before the front door of the castle. A few moments later she found herself swept up in a tide completely beyond her control, as she was introduced to a horde of complete strangers. How was it possible for anyone to have so many relations? she wondered, while being introduced to a bewildering number of countless aunts, uncles and distant cousins.

She had just been talking to someone's great-great-grandfather, who was, he informed her proudly, well over one hundred years of age, when she turned her head to see a glamorous figure moving in her direction.

Quite *why* she should have forgotten that Désirée was so startlingly beautiful, she had no idea. Or why it hadn't occurred to her that since the other woman's father was a neighbouring landowner Xavier's ex-girlfriend was almost bound to have been asked to the reception. As Désirée wafted towards her, in a hot-pink dress which seemed glued to her voluptuous figure, Louisa braced herself for the confrontation.

But the Frenchwoman was not, it seemed, intent on causing trouble.

'I had to come today—if only to offer you my deep apologies,' she said in a low voice, putting a small, delicate hand on Louisa's arm, and leading her to the side of the room. 'I'm really ashamed of how badly I behaved, the other day. It was just the shock, you understand. . .?' She gave a helpless shrug of her delicate shoulders. 'But it was also very stupid. After all, most of the women here are secretly in love with Xavier. And it isn't difficult to see why,' she added with a low, rueful laugh as she turned to glance across the room at his tall, handsome figure. 'So I hope that you will forgive me?'

Louisa suddenly felt ashamed of how she had mis-judged this woman. Désirée had, after all, only con-firmed her own fears about marrying such an outstandingly attractive, virile man. And it must have taken some considerable courage to have offered such an abject apology.

'Thank you for. . .well, I'm glad you came today,' she told Désirée. 'I hope we can be friends. You're just about the only person I know here. In fact, I was terrified of having to meet so many complete strangers,' she admitted with a nervous smile.

'Yes, I can see it must be difficult.' Désirée nodded. 'I suppose the last time there was such a family gathering must have been when his great-uncle threw a big reception for Xavier's marriage to Georgette. Of course,' she added hurriedly, 'that *was* a long time ago. So you don't need to worry that he might still be carrying a torch for Georgette. I'm sure that he now only has eyes for you!'

She knew it was asking for trouble, but Louisa couldn't seem to prevent herself from saying, 'What was Georgette really like? I mean,' she added with a careless laugh, as if she really wasn't at all concerned, 'everyone keeps telling me that she was so beautiful and lovely, but I just wondered if——'

'Oh, yes, I'm afraid she was.' Désirée gave an envious sigh. 'Absolutely *stunning*! And, as you might expect, Xavier was *crazy* about her. When she acciden-tally killed herself, on one of these mountain roads. . . well, we all thought that he'd go out of his mind with grief. He shut himself away in that huge apartment in Paris, and for years he just concentrated on work and his business affairs. In fact,' Désirée confided in a low voice, 'I really don't think that he's ever really recovered from her death. He certainly won't ever have her name mentioned in his presence. But as I said, I'm sure you haven't any *real* need to worry.' She gave the tall English girl a consoling pat on her arm. 'I am sure he won't be making comparisons between you and Georgette.'

But she obviously thinks he *will*! Louisa told herself dismally as the other woman gave her a soft, sympathetic smile, before drifting away to talk to some friends.

Left standing alone for a few moments at the side of the room, Louisa felt her trembling legs nearly give way under the weight of her deep despair and desolation. How could she possibly compete with a legendary beauty like the lovely Georgette? A woman whose loss had caused Xavier years of grief, and whose memory was — as Désirée clearly believed — still vividly alive in his heart.

CHAPTER TEN

EVENTUALLY, of course, like all bad dreams, the interminably long wedding reception slowly came to an end. Replete with food and wine, as well as having had the opportunity to catch up with all the latest island gossip, the guests slowly departed.

However, Louisa was shocked when Marie-Thérèse also announced her intention of leaving. Especially as the girl seemed to have organised a whole fleet of willing young men, who were busy carrying an amazing amount of luggage down the wide oak staircase.

When Xavier loudly demanded to know what was going on, his niece laughingly informed him that she was flying off to Paris. 'Two's company—three's a crowd!' she added firmly. 'And while Tante Sophie has her own wing in the castle, *I* don't want to have to sit twiddling my thumbs while you two lovebirds "bill and coo" at each other.'

How wrong can you be? Louisa thought unhappily, before trying to persuade the young girl to change her mind. But her intentions were frustrated by Xavier, who surprised her by not only agreeing with his niece, but also suggesting that it was about time she found her own apartment in Paris.

'My thoughts exactly!' Marie-Thérèse laughed, throwing her arms about his neck and giving him a hug, before planting a quick kiss on Louisa's pale cheek. 'I'm, sure that my uncle truly loves you—so relax and be happy!' the girl whispered hurriedly in her ear, before rushing out to join the friends who'd agreed to take her to the airport.

Louisa felt bereft and lonely as she waved goodbye to Marie-Thérèse. They'd become good friends, and the castle would now seem a lonely place without her.

'Well, Madame la Comtesse—and what do you suppose we ought to do now, hmm?' Xavier drawled, as

142

the last cars left the castle forecourt, and Tante Sophie staggered off to her own suite of rooms, triumphantly happy that all her arrangements for the wedding reception had gone so well.

'I don't really know,' she muttered nervously. It was only late afternoon, and the whole evening seemed to stretch out in front of her, like a life sentence. 'I would like — um — I would like to take this dress off, and get into something more comfortable — like a pair of jeans. And then we could maybe — er — maybe go for a walk?' she suggested wildly.

'Yes, indeed we could,' Xavier agreed blandly, placing an arm casually about her waist, and leading her up the stairs. 'However, I can see that you are feeling tired and uncomfortable in your wedding-dress. So, why do we not start with removing that garment — and then see where we go from there?'

'We. . .?' she echoed nervously. 'There's really no need. . . I mean, I'm quite capable of undoing my own zip!'

'Of course you are,' he agreed again, in the same bland voice which he'd used earlier, as he led her reluctant figure into his bedroom suite. Only now that she was standing so close to him, she could see an unmistakable gleam of amusement in his dark eyes. 'However, it does seem a pity not to accept the aid of your new husband, hmm?'

'Yes, well. . .' she muttered, wondering what on earth to say next, and trying to ignore the huge, spectacularly draped bed, which unfortunately seemed to dominate the room. Equally unfortunate, it now appeared, was the fact that she'd had so much else occupying her mind during the run-up to the wedding that she hadn't given any thought to her future sleeping arrangements. Was she *really* expected to share that truly amazing bed with Xavier?

'I think you'll find that it's surprisingly comfortable,' he murmured, accurately reading her mind as she stared at the enormous piece of furniture in awed fascination. 'Come and see,' he added, firmly leading her trembling figure across the soft carpet.

'But. . .but it's far too early to go to bed!' she exclaimed helplessly. There was nothing she could do to prevent her cheeks from flushing a deep crimson as he gave a low, husky laugh, stripping off the jacket of his beautifully tailored dark suit, and tossing it carelessly on a nearby chair.

'Really Louisa!' he grinned, removing his tie and loosening the buttons of his shirt, before pulling her into his arms. 'Do you think there's some kind of law which says I can only make love to my wife in the dark?'

'No, of course I don't,' she snapped nervously, trying to tear her eyes away from the curly dark hair on his chest. With a heavy heart, she realised that it was no good trying to prevaricate. She was just going to have to 'own up' and tell him the truth. 'The fact is. . .well, for some reason you seem to think. . . I mean, I'm not nearly as experienced or sophisticated as you ——'

'Hush, *chérie*, there is no need for these explanations,' he murmured, raising a hand to gently brush a stray coil of hair from her flushed cheek. 'I already know that you are not an experienced woman of the world.'

'How can you possibly know that?'

He smiled ruefully down into her green eyes. 'Because, my darling—I regret to say that I *am* an experienced man of the world.'

'But ——'

'I knew from the moment when I first held you in my arms,' he told her firmly, before giving an expressive shrug of his broad shoulders. 'It was obvious, from your almost virginal response to my embrace, that you were unused to such encounters. Or—if I were to put it more crudely—that you were not a woman given to "sleeping around".'

'Well, it's not exactly a *crime* to be so inexperienced!' she told him huffily, well aware that she wasn't being logical, but feeling deeply embarrassed at this frank discussion about her lack of sexual expertise.

'*Au contraire*,' Xavier said firmly. 'Any man, however old-fashioned it may be, would wish his wife to be pure in heart and deed. In fact, that is one of the reasons why I felt in honour bound to marry you.'

Louisa stared at him, the blood draining from her face as she finally accepted the truth: this rivetingly attractive, handsome man really *had* gone through the wedding ceremony today simply to protect both his reputation and hers!

With a sharp, animal cry of pain she wrenched herself from his arms, sobbing as if her heart would break, as she fled into the bathroom. Tearing off the hideously expensive wedding-dress, which she *never* wanted to see again, she leaned weeping against the cold marble walls, which seemed to have no effect in cooling down her heated flesh.

How *could* she have been so stupid? How could she have married a man who clearly felt nothing but pity towards her — *plus* an overriding sense of duty, of course, she reminded herself bitterly, as tears of misery flooded down her cheeks. But he'd never said that he loved her. It was solely her own hopeless passion which had so *stupidly* led her to hope against hope that he might. . .possibly — come to care for her.

Her distraught thoughts were interrupted by a loud bang on the door.

'Come out of there — immediately!' Xavier demanded loudly. 'I can promise you, I'll break the door down if you don't!' he added in a dangerously threatening voice, which left no doubt that he meant exactly what he said.

Brushing the weak tears from her eyes, she slowly unlocked the door, her slim figure, in a diaphanous petticoat, presenting a forlorn picture as she stood trembling in the doorway.

'Ah, Louisa. . .' he whispered, gently taking her quivering figure into his arms. 'I can't possibly have my sweet bride in tears — not on her wedding-day! Did you *really* think that I married you just because I wished to preserve your honour?' he added lifting her up in his arms, and carrying her over to the enormous bed.

'Y-yes. . .' she sniffed, burying her face in his

shoulder for a moment, before she found herself being lowered down on to the soft mattress.

'Have you forgotten that I told you *just* how deeply attracted I was to you? Did I not admit that I could hardly keep my hands off you. . .?' he added in a soft murmur, gently tilting her face up towards him.

Louisa felt suddenly breathless, her heart thudding and pounding as she glimpsed the naked desire gleaming in the dark eyes now staring down at her so intently. Leaning weakly against his broad chest, and savouring the warmth of his body through his thin silk shirt, she quivered in response as his hands began to caress the soft curves of her body.

'Believe me, *ma chérie*, I desire you with all the force and hunger that a man can feel for a woman,' he breathed huskily, his fingers moving to brush the thin straps of the petticoat off her slim shoulders. 'How can you doubt my feelings?' he added thickly as he exposed the burgeoning fullness of her breasts to his view.

'But you never said. . . I mean——'

'Hush, my sweet one. This is no time for talking. . . not when I can feast my eyes on your loveliness, your soft, velvety skin the colour of pure alabaster. . .so pure and untouched. . .'

His hoarse whispers seemed to dramatically inflame her emotions, sending shivers tingling down her spine as his soft caresses became more insistent and more possessive. The scorching touch of his lips seemed to ignite a flame deep inside her, and not only did she rapidly seem to lose all sense of time and place, but the hard warmth of his tanned body and the unbelievable ecstasy engendered by his sensual mouth and hands, moving so erotically over her soft flesh, seemed to lift her into a completely different world.

Never, in her wildest dreams, could she have ever envisaged such mind-blowing sensations, the release of such an overwhelming torrent of passion and love as she felt for this man. Never before had she been touched like this, nor believed that someone could be so completely the master of all her heart's desire.

With her flesh almost melting beneath his intimate

caresses, she sank beneath the ever increasing waves of
throbbing desire, hardly hearing the deep groan torn
from his throat as she instinctively moved wantonly
and sensually beneath him. Her mind and body spinning totally out of control, she was completely unaware
of the increasing urgency of his own passion, unaware,
even, of crying out loud with rapturous joy and delight,
as at last he brought them both to an earth-shattering
peak of mutual ecstasy.

She seemed to have lost all sense of time, Louisa
thought, pouring herself another cup of coffee. The
morning mist was shrouding the far mountain peaks,
but it looked as if it was going to be another hot and
sunny day.

Was it four or six weeks since her wedding in the
town hall at Corte? It somehow seemed a lifetime
away, with the succeeding days and weeks merging into
one another, like a stream of shimmering pearls on a
long thread of happiness.

And, quite amazingly, she really *was* happy! Given
the stress and strain leading up to her forced marriage,
it seemed incredible that she should now be sitting
here, on the terrace outside the dining-room of the
castle, and almost sighing with pleasure as she gazed at
the magnificent view spread out before her. And she
had to admit that most, if not all the credit for her
present state of contentment must go to Xavier. Very
slowly and cautiously, it seemed, he had gradually
relaxed his guard, allowing her to see occasional
glimpses of a much warmer and softer personality
which lay beneath the hard, tough and arrogant character which he normally presented to the world.

Of course, he was never going to come to love her
as much as she loved him, Louisa acknowledged with a
deep pang of sadness, as she rose and walked over to
the stone balustrade edging the terrace. It would be a
miracle if he did, and she had long since given up belief
in any such childish fantasy. In fact, she'd forced herself
to accept that maybe such a hard, forceful businessman
simply wasn't able to give her his 'love' — or not what

she understood by the word. But in all other respects there was no denying the fact that Xavier was proving to be a warm and caring husband.

It was embarrassing to remember just how incredibly ignorant she'd been. No romantic novels that she'd read had, in any way, prepared her for the sensual delight and rapture which she'd experienced night after night during these past weeks.

Closing her eyes for a moment, she savoured the soft morning breeze on her flushed cheeks; her nostrils filled with the sharp, pungent scent of pine trees and the sweet smell of wild lavender, rising from the valley far below.

In accusing Xavier of lust, and claiming that it could be no basis for a marriage, she'd had no idea of the ecstatic, magical intensity of feelings which seemed to flare into life whenever he touched her. Lust might have been the driving force behind his apparently insatiable desire for her body. However, the nights they'd spent locked in each other's arms in that amazing bed had been ones of such spellbinding, sweet enchantment that she had many times found herself weeping with joy and happiness.

And it wasn't just the nights. Even Tante Sophie had been surprised at how often Xavier had demanded that she accompany him on his various trips about the island. The sight of rugged bare rocks, tumbling down the hillsides, and the lakes and mountain streams full of trout, the long, sun-baked beaches of white-gold sand at Porto Vecchio, and the charming and relaxed atmosphere of the small Mediterranean fishing port at Ile Rousse, had given her fresh insights into Corsican life. But it was the time they'd spent alone together on those journeys — talking about everything under the sun — which had also come to mean so much to her.

Despite the seeds of doubt planted by Désirée at the wedding reception, Xavier had never made any reference to his first wife. All reason and logic told her that she was undoubtedly living in a fool's paradise — that if he was comparing her to the lovely Georgette it could only be to her detriment. But with Xavier's obvious care and kind concern that she should be happy, Louisa found she had no will or desire to do anything other than to accept her fate, quite unable to prevent herself from loving him with all her heart.

The sound of quick footsteps across the terrace made her turn her head to see Tante Sophie approaching, waving a piece of paper in her hand.

'I've just heard from Marie-Thérèse,' the old lady exclaimed. 'She tells me that she has found a nice apartment in Paris, and — I can hardly believe it! — she's about to enrol at the university, for a course in fine arts.'

'That sounds like a good idea.'

'Yes, indeed. It will be much better for her to be with people of her own age.' Tante Sophie nodded vigorously. 'My nephew has been a wonderful uncle and guardian, of course, but it took him far too long to realise that the girl had become a young woman. And when Marie-Thérèse told me that Xavier had been insisting that she marry your stepbrother. . .' She sighed and shook her head. 'Have you heard from your brother lately?'

'Yes, I was talking to him on the phone only a day or two ago. He tells me that he's going to work for the American branch of his bank, in New York.'

And that *had* to be a good idea, Louisa told herself, recalling how she'd finally rung Jamie after her wedding, to explain the full background to everything that had happened ever since she'd arrived in Corsica. He'd been surprised, of course, but she had been touched by his unexpected concern for her future welfare. Louisa wasn't at all sure that she'd managed to convince her stepbrother that Comte Cinarchesi was *not* a wicked old man who was holding her a prisoner here in the castle, like one of Bluebeard's wives.

'But what about your job, Lou?' he'd asked. 'You've always been such a career girl. I hope you've made the right decision.'

Louisa, who knew that she'd had little or nothing to do with the 'decision' — which had been prompted more by her own errant emotions than by any hard and sensible logic — had merely murmured some platitudes, before asking about his future plans. When he explained that, following his marriage to Sonia Armstrong, he was going to take up Lord Armstrong's offer of a job in the American office, Louisa had silently applauded her future sister-in-law. She'd always thought that Sonia had seemed to be a very sensible, down-to-earth girl, and it now looked as though she was right. Removing Jamie well away from his old haunts and bad habits could only be a good idea!

'I've never been to America,' Tante Sophie was saying wistfully as she sat down and began rummaging through her large handbag, before producing some small empty bottles.

Louisa smiled to herself as she watched the old lady. Although Xavier's aunt wasn't exactly ancient, she'd openly expressed her firm intention of living to well over a hundred years of age. And, if the success of her aim could be accurately measured by the amazing number of pills, potions and assorted medicines which she took every day, Tante Sophie seemed to be well on the way to achieving her target!

'What on earth were these for?' Louisa picked up a bottle bearing an obscure Latin inscription.

'My dear — they're absolutely *vital*! I really don't think my liver will continue to function properly without them,' Tante Sophie told her earnestly. 'So, if you're going with Xavier to Bastia today, could you please buy me some more from the chemist?'

Louisa, who had been feeling rather tired and listless over the past week, had decided to spend a quiet, lazy day at the castle. However, since Aunt Sophie was liable to fret herself into a state without the security blanket of all her favourite pills, maybe she ought to go to Bastia with Xavier after all?

'All right, Tante, I'll pick up some more for you this afternoon.'

'It might be a good idea if you also got a tonic for yourself,' the old woman told her, peering up at the girl. 'You've been looking just a little peaky lately, and

I noticed that you didn't eat much dinner last night —
or any breakfast this morning, for that matter.'

'I just don't seem to be hungry at the moment. And
no,' she added quickly, as the other woman looked at
her in alarm, clearly frightened of catching some con-
tagious disease. 'I'm quite well. Just feeling a little
tired, that's all.'

Tante Sophie pursed her lips and shook her head.
'All the same, I think you ought to see a doctor. You
seem far too pale, and it's very important to keep in
good health.'

Sitting in the car beside Xavier, as he drove them
north towards the town of Bastia, which lay on the east
coast of the Cap Corse, Louisa realised that maybe it
hadn't been such a good idea to have volunteered to
fetch Tante Sophie's medicines. Once again she seemed
to be feeling. . .well, not exactly sick, but very slightly
nauseous.

'Are you feeling all right?' Xavier gave her a quick
glance of concern. 'You are looking a bit pale.'

'I'm fine,' she told him firmly. 'Although I hope you
aren't becoming obsessed with health matters, like your
aunt!'

Xavier laughed. 'I'm not sure whether Tante Sophie
is so fit *because* of, or despite all those pills! Maybe I
should buy some shares in her favourite pharmaceutical
company?'

'Since so many people are now living to a great age,
it would probably be a good investment,' Louisa muttered, leaning back on her seat and relishing the
warmth of the sun on her face. It was strange how tired
she was feeling these days. Maybe it wouldn't be the
end of the world if she just closed her eyes for a few
minutes. . .?

Unfortunately, it wasn't just a few minutes. When
she woke up, Louisa was ashamed to discover that
she'd slept for most of the journey.

'I'm not at all surprised,' Xavier told her with a grin.
'With so much — er — exercise at night, it is not at all
strange that you should feel a need to sleep during
the day!'

Louisa's cheeks reddened. 'What nonsense! And if that's the reason—you certainly ought to be feeling even more tired than I do!'

He grinned. 'Ah-ha. . .but, you see, *I'm* an incredibly fit—not to say extremely vigorous—demon lover!'

'You're also extremely arrogant, and appear to be suffering from a swollen head!' she told him sternly, her efforts to keep a straight face frustrated by Xavier's infectious rumble of laughter, as he drove them through the tunnel which ran under the ancient Citadelle and old port to enter the ancient town of Bastia.

After explaining that he was paying a visit to an elderly gentleman, who'd been the main trustee of his great-uncle's estate, Xavier dropped her off in the Boulevard Paoli, instructing her to take a taxi and join him at an address in the old part of the town when she'd done her shopping.

After purchasing Tante Sophie's pills, Louisa noticed that there was a doctor's surgery practically next door to the pharmacy. And, deciding that possibly Tante was right, and that it wouldn't do her any harm to have a physical check-up, she rang the bell.

Yes, it was possible for the doctor to see her straight-away. And 'Yes,' he told her some twenty minutes later, 'I am happy to inform you, *madame*, that you are expecting a baby. I will have to carry out some tests, of course.' The doctor shrugged, before giving her a beaming smile. 'But I'm quite certain that you are about to make your husband a very happy man!'

When looking back on that day, there seemed to be some complete blanks in her mind. Louisa could never remember how or why, some considerable time later, she found herself sitting outside a café, under the plane trees in the Place St-Nicholas, staring blindly at a glass of cold lemonade. Her mind in a complete daze, she barely saw or heard the waiters skilfully dodging the traffic as they pirouetted back and forth across the road with loaded trays of drinks and pastries.

Just how happy Xavier would be, she had no idea. All Louisa knew was that *she* felt completely *shattered*!

Far from being either pleased or sorry, her predominant emotion was one of total shock. It just wasn't. . . well, it was the one thing to which she had given absolutely no thought before marrying Xavier. He'd mentioned that he wanted a family, of course, but that had seemed so far in the future that it wasn't something that she'd even considered.

Leaning back in her chair, Louisa placed a shaking, tentative hand on her stomach. She was certain that she didn't look pregnant. She definitely didn't *feel* pregnant. Could the doctor have been wrong? Maybe it was just possible that he'd made a mistake — and she *wasn't* pregnant, after all. If so, it might be better if she didn't say anything to Xavier — not just at the moment, she told herself, her brain a mass of contradictory emotions as she tried to stop her body from tembling with shock and dismay.

It wasn't that she had anything against babies — she simply didn't know the first thing about them. In fact, she'd never really thought about having her *own* children. It had always seemed such a remote possibility, something she might eventually get around to, if and when she got married after achieving a successful career. But now. . .? Now that her career had been so abruptly terminated, and she was married to Xavier. . .? Well, it was just too much to take in straight away.

Eventually managing to pull herself partially together, Louisa hailed a taxi. On her arrival, she didn't have the chance to say anything as Xavier, after bidding farewell to his old friend, insisted that he wanted to take her out for an early meal before the journey home to the castle.

Preoccupied with her own distraught thoughts, Louisa was faintly surprised to find herself being led inside a rough-looking tavern, its dark, smoke-filled interior not at all the type of place which Xavier usually liked to patronise.

However, after they'd been taken to their table, and he'd ordered for her a bowl of *ziminu* — a local fish soup, sprinkled with croutons and finely grated, hard local cheese — she was slowly beginning to feel marginally better. But only *marginally*, she thought, sitting silent and bemused as Xavier explained that he hoped they'd have the opportunity, that evening, of hearing the *paghiella*.

It was, he informed her, a quite unique and very ancient form of traditional Corsican singing, performed by male voices. 'Although a considerable effort has been made to revive the technique, it is rarely heard nowadays, except in the more remote parts of the island.'

Louisa tried to concentrate on what he was saying. But she couldn't seem to absorb anything, except a dreadful thought which had just exploded like a time bomb in her confused brain. Because, if she *was* pregnant, that meant that she was now completely and utterly *trapped*!

It was far too late now to chastise herself for being such a fool, too late to rail at herself for not giving any thought to the necessity for birth control. That was her problem, and had nothing to do with the baby. Besides, now that she'd had a few hours to think about it, she was surprised to find how much she wanted to have Xavier's child. But what about the future? With despair, she realised that she now had no choice in the matter. She was irrevocably trapped and totally committed — both by her love for Xavier *and* the coming birth of a child — to marriage with a man who didn't love her!

In the darkened, smoky atmosphere, deeply preoccupied with her own miserable thoughts, it was some time before Louisa realised that Xavier was drawing her attention to three heavily built young men standing at a bar on the far side of the room. After draining their glasses, they positioned themselves side by side, each with his elbow resting on the shoulder of the man next to him, before they all took a breath and began to sing.

Louisa sat transfixed as the three strong voices — baritone, bass and tenor — rose and fell in a harsh sequence of notes, the deliberately discordant, clashing music sounding like a primitive, war-like incantation which was, at one and the same time, far more agonisingly poignant and bitter than the lament sung at Oletta.

It was totally absorbing. She'd never heard *anything* like the sound of these three young men, their swaying bodies pressed closely together, as though they were a single instrument. The sound they produced was at once heart-wrenching, and yet mysterious, as if it alone held the key to some long-lost, ancient secret from the dawn of time.

And it was, it seemed, a song without end. The men's voices, almost drowned at the end of each stanza by loud and heavy applause, merely took up the theme again and again, their voices gathering force as the extraordinarily melodic yet harshly clashing sounds faded away, only to rise again once more.

She found herself, along with the rest of the audience, completely caught up in a strange and wild euphoria — almost a feeling of mass hysteria — as they all seemed to become one with the singers and the song.

Louisa was still in a complete trance when she found Xavier helping her from her seat, and escorting her out of the restaurant.

'I'm pleased you were able to hear the *paghiella*, but it is time we were going home,' he told her, as she stared up at him with dazed eyes, 'Hearing such music can be an unforgettable experience, *n'est-ce pas*?'

Louisa could only nod, a deep lump in her throat preventing her from saying anything. And possibly Xavier was right. Maybe it was because the music had been so emotionally charged, or it could have been just too much for her to cope with, on top of the other major event of that traumatic day. Whatever the reason, after travelling home in silence, Louisa suddenly found her slim frame unable to combat a heavy storm of grief, desolation and overwhelming distress, which caused her to burst out weeping as Xavier led her into the great hall of the castle.

'Louisa! What on earth is wrong?' he demanded

anxiously as she took to her heels, dashing up the wide staircase towards their bedroom.

'Please, Louisa — you will make yourself ill!' He frowned down at her as she lay huddled on the bed. 'What reason can you have for such distress?' Not knowing how to explain her extraordinary mixture and turmoil of emotions — mainly because she really didn't understand them herself — Louisa could only silently shake her head, grateful to accept Xavier's handkerchief to stem the weak tears still trickling down her cheeks.

'Come! You must give me an explanation why you feel such obvious pain and sorrow,' he demanded forcefully, putting his hand on her shoulder and giving her a rough shake.

'I don't know. . .' she wailed helplessly. And then, from among the various emotions surging through her mind and body, she suddenly found herself saying, 'I saw a doctor today. . . He told me that. . .it seems I'm going to have a baby!'

'*My child*?'

'It certainly isn't anyone else's!' she cried, burying her face in the pillow, her body racked with sobs.

'You do not want this child? Can it really cause you such grief and agony of mind?' he asked, his voice suddenly sounding cold and bitter.

'Yes. . .no — I don't know!' she wailed helplessly.

'You don't find it very "chic" to have a baby? Or are you worried about losing your figure?' he demanded scornfully, the scathing note in his voice seeming to echo loudly around the room.

'No!' She raised her head to gaze up at him in bewilderment. 'No. . .you don't understand. . .'

'Oh, yes, unfortunately, I *understand* only too well!' Xavier gave a cruel laugh, rising to his feet and glaring down with a hard, ruthless expression. 'You may not want my child, but that — Madame wife — that is just *too bad*!' he ground out through clenched teeth, before striding across the bedroom to the door, and slamming it loudly behind him.

CHAPTER ELEVEN

LOUISA had no doubt that the four weeks following her visit to Bastia were quite the most unhappy ones of her entire life.

Ever since Xavier had stormed out of the bedroom that evening, she'd seen virtually nothing of her husband. It was as though his slamming of the bedroom door had been a symbolic act — a final, dramatic gesture signalling the end of her all too brief marriage. And whereas she had once spent her nights clasped in the warmth and security of her husband's arms, she now lay forlornly alone in the enormous bed, weeping copious tears of anguish and desolation.

Quite where Xavier spent his nights, she had no idea. Her pride alone — if nothing else — prevented her from enquiring too closely as to his exact whereabouts. However, from something Tante Sophie had let slip, she suspected that he was now spending most of his time in Paris.

Exactly *why* he was avoiding her like this, she had absolutely no idea. Trailing listlessly through the countless beautifully decorated but empty rooms of the huge castle, she completely failed to find the answer. With her head pounding and throbbing from tension headaches during the day, and the loneliness of her many sleepless nights, she couldn't think of any sane, sensible reason why he should be deliberately avoiding all contact with her. And when Louisa compared her present bleak, sterile existence with the ecstatic happiness she'd so briefly discovered in Xavier's arms, she wept many tears of misery and grief.

Surely, she told herself, it couldn't be *that* unusual for a new bride to be dismayed and upset on discovering a pregnancy which had been neither planned nor thought about in any detail? Now that she'd had the time to become used to the idea of a baby — the fact

157

having been confirmed by Tante Sophie's own doctor —
Louisa was becoming thrilled and excited at the
thought of giving birth to a child. Or she *would* have
been, if it wasn't for Xavier's cruel and quite inexplicable behaviour.

There was no denying that she'd panicked, behaving
more like a frightened child than an adult, on first
learning of her pregnancy. She was also certain that
the heart-rending music of the *paghiella* — an overwhelming emotional experience — had merely com-
pounded the problem, pushing her already sorely tried
nervous system temporarily out of control.

While Louisa normally prided herself on having a
healthy, sceptical attitude towards so-called 'psycho-
logical' problems, it didn't take a genius to realise that
she'd been under considerable stress and strain ever
since she'd arrived in Corsica. First of all, in meeting
and falling madly in love with Xavier, and then — even
though she knew he didn't love her — being swayed by
her own weak frailty into a forced marriage, simply
because she couldn't help herself. So no wonder, when
she'd found herself so unexpectedly pregnant, that
she'd temporarily flipped her lid! And, while it was
something that she desperately regretted, she still
couldn't understand Xavier's reaction. Surely an
experienced and sophisticated man of thirty-five, who'd
also been married before, should have been able to
understand that she'd been merely suffering from a
temporary crisis of nerves?

Maybe, if she'd been able to talk honestly to him,
Xavier might have understood that it wasn't just the
unexpected news of the baby which had thrown her so
completely. But since he'd virtually disappeared from
her life, and was clearly making absolutely certain that
they had no opportunity to communicate with one
another, there was nothing she could do to rectify the
increasingly grim situation.

It seemed to Louisa that she had now become a
totally abandoned, wretched prisoner in this huge
castle, a lonely prison from which there seemed no
escape. In fact, if it hadn't been for Rosa and Tante

Sophie, she was certain that she would have gone completely out of her mind.

On discovering the news of her pregnancy from Xavier's aunt, the housekeeper had clasped the Comte's new wife to her massive bosom in a warm hug. She'd been fussing around Louisa ever since, producing wonderful meals to try to tempt the girl's evident lack of appetite, and doing everything she could to make her feel as comfortable as possible.

Tante Sophie, too, was clearly fascinated by the forthcoming birth of a baby. 'There hasn't been a child here at the castle for at least a hundred years,' she informed Louisa. 'And while I must admit that I know nothing about babies, it will certainly be an interesting experience!'

It was Tante Sophie, of course, who after a long talk with her doctor had insisted on a healthy *régime* for the expectant mother. Disappointed to discover that, nowadays, pregnant women were advised to take as few medicines as possible, she nevertheless supervised Louisa's diet with an eagle eye, as well as making sure that she had plenty of healthy exercise.

It was after those daily afternoon walks upon which Tante Sophie and her doctor set so much store that she would join the elderly woman for a cup of English tea in the elegantly decorated main *salon* of the castle. It was there, amid the teacups, that Tante Sophie liked to reminisce about the past. And while they were both very careful not to discuss Xavier's present behaviour—clearly a cause of great embarrassment to his aunt—Louisa did gain some insight into his family history, which might have done much to forge the hard, tough personality of her husband.

As Tante Sophie romantically pointed out, Xavier had a considerable amount in common with that famous Corsican, Napoléon Bonaparte. They had both, it seemed, come from good but impoverished backgrounds, with each determined to make his own way in the world. Again, like Napoléon, Xavier had gone to France as a young man, to make his fortune—

an aim in which he'd succeeded beyond everyone's wildest dreams.

'Xavier's father—a dear man who died far too young—would have been *so* proud of his son,' Tante Sophie told her. 'Of course, no one *ever* expected so many members of the family to die without leaving male heirs—or that Xavier would eventually inherit the title of Comte Cinarchesi. It certainly put the snooty noses of our French relations well out of joint!' the old lady chuckled, before explaining that there were two branches of the family, both descended from a Corsican general who'd fought alongside Napoléon, gaining considerable money and land throughout France in the process. It seemed that Xavier's rather grand French relatives, who still lived on what was left of their vast country estates, in the Dordogne, had taken little or no interest in Xavier.

'They treated the poor, fatherless boy quite disgracefully!' Tante Sophie exclaimed, still obviously feeling indignant all these years later. 'They did nothing to help him get started in life, and although he is now extremely wealthy it has been solely due to his own ability and talent for business. But I have to admit,' the old lady sighed, 'that, having been forced to work so extremely hard, early in his life, Xavier may appear to be rather difficult and—er—fierce at times.'

Tante Sophie's voice had been full of warmth and pride when speaking about her nephew, whom she obviously adored. And she was clearly doing her best to offer a partial explanation for his hard, ruthless personality.

'Well, for a man who's supposed to be such a whiz at business, he doesn't appear to have much luck with his wives!' Louisa pointed out bitterly.

It was one of those days when she was feeling particularly low and sorry for herself, although she knew it wasn't fair to take her unhappiness out on Tante Sophie. However, she was soon punished for her flip remark, when the elderly woman hastened to set the record straight.

'His wife's tragic death was hardly Xavier's fault,'

she said firmly. 'Georgette could be volatile and head-strong, maybe even just a little spoilt. But everyone always forgave her those small faults, because she was so very beautiful.' The old lady gave a heavy sigh. 'It was truly a dark day. . .a terrible tragedy when she was killed in that dreadful car accident.'

'Is *that* why Franco, the chauffeur, has been given express instructions that I'm not allowed to drive any of the cars in the garage?' Louisa asked, her voice sounding harsher than she intended, but she was always disturbed and upset at being forced to listen to yet more praise for the beautiful Georgette. Although she needed no convincing that Xavier's first wife had been a pearl beyond price, it seemed as though the dead woman's ghost was now beginning to haunt her days, as well as her nights.

'Oh, no. I'm sure it's just my nephew's concern for your safety,' Tante Sophie hastily assured her. But Louisa didn't believe a word of it. With Xavier's obvious lack of interest in her, he'd probably be only too glad if she wrote herself off in a car accident, she told herself miserably.

Knowing that she was virtually a prisoner here at the castle, and that she couldn't go on living this isolated, twilight life for much longer, Louisa was getting to the point when she was going to have to admit defeat. It was clearly foolish to keep on hoping that Xavier would break his ominous silence — that he'd suddenly appear, and explain the reason for the harsh abandonment of his new wife.

However, although he may have intended to make sure that she saw no one, other than Tante Sophie, he evidently hadn't taken into account his ex-girlfriend, Désirée.

Quite why the glamorous French woman had suddenly appeared, a week ago, and continued to pay almost daily calls to the castle, was beyond her comprehension.

She knew very well that Désirée was still carrying a torch for Xavier, and quite unable to understand why he'd married the English girl, in preference to herself.

But what she hoped to gain by insisting on being Louisa's 'friend', and always harping on about the manifold virtues of Xavier's dead wife, she had no idea.

However, it soon transpired that this morning's visit from Désirée was more than just a casual call.

'All alone — *again*?' Désirée exclaimed, accompanying her words with a brilliant smile as she joined Louisa out on the terrace.

It's that awful smile of hers that I can't stand! Louisa suddenly found herself thinking. It was that blindingly false smile, never quite reflected in the hard, glittering dark eyes, which always triggered alarm bells in her mind.

'Now that we've become such *good* friends, I felt I had to come and see you today,' Désirée said, in a sickly-sweet voice. 'I had hoped. . . I mean, when I saw poor Xavier in Paris a week ago. . .well, I knew then that things weren't going too well with your marriage.' She paused, giving a sorrowful shake of her dark head.

'I didn't know that you'd seen Xavier.' Louisa frowned.

'Well, I didn't want to upset you, did I?' Désirée looked at her with pity. 'But from what he was saying on the phone last night. . .' She shrugged her shoulders.

'He. . .he telephoned you. . .?' Louisa stared at her, feeling as though she'd been hit by a heavy sandbag.

'Why not? We've known each other all our lives, haven't we? Of course, poor Xavier feels *very* guilty. He knows that it's all his fault, of course. The fact that he can't bring himself to. . .well, we're both adults, Louisa. It's very sad, but I did warn you, didn't I?'

'Warn me. . .?' Louisa echoed weakly, feeling like a helpless rabbit trapped in the full glare of a car's headlamps, but powerless to do anything about it.

Désirée gave another sorrowful shake of her head. 'There was *always* going to be the problem of Georgette,' she pointed out, her tone suggesting that she was talking to a particularly dim-witted child. 'And now poor Xavier has found out, when it's far too late, that he just can't forget her. After all, why else should he be avoiding you?'

Why else? Louisa agreed silently, her heart leaden with despair. Despite what he'd said to her about wanting a family, when it came to the point, Xavier obviously just couldn't face the thought of having a child — not by a wife he didn't love.

It was then that Louisa realised that she had no alternative but to leave the castle as quickly as possible. A conclusion echoed by Désirée, whose voice seemed to be coming from a long distance away.

'There really isn't any point in your hanging around here at the castle, is there?' she was saying. 'If it were *me* — I'd be on the next aeroplane to England. But then, *I* have a great deal of pride! I couldn't *bear* to be married to a man who didn't love me.'

Désirée, her voice hard and spiteful, had swiftly tossed aside all pretence of 'friendship', and was now gazing at the English girl with an obvious sneer on her face.

She only had herself to blame, Louisa thought, a rising tide of anger at her own folly beginning to sweep aside the sluggish apathy in her mind. After all, Xavier had never lied to her. He'd never said that he loved her. And therefore their marriage — built on such flimsy, shallow foundations — was bound to have disintegrated eventually, even if he hadn't still been in love with his dead wife.

'It's so sad,' Désirée murmured, in in sickly-false voice. 'I only wish I could do something. . .'

Louisa rose slowly and wearily from her chair. 'Yes, there is something you can do for me. You can tell "poor" Xavier that he has no need to feel guilty. I should never have married him in the first place. As for the future. . .' She took a deep breath, before adding grimly, '*If* he bothers to ask, you can tell him that both I and the baby will do very well without him!'

'The. . .the *baby*!' Désirée gasped, clearly stunned as she stared at the other girl in open-mouthed shock

and dismay. 'You're expecting a *baby*. . .? I didn't
know. . . Are you sure. . .?'

'Of course I'm sure!' Louisa snapped, suddenly
feeling tired to death of the whole charade as she
turned to go into the castle. 'I don't know why Xavier
hasn't told you about the baby—but that's his problem.
I suggest you let yourself out,' she added over her
shoulder, leaving the other girl's rigid, shocked figure
alone on the terrace.

It was sheer anger at both her own stupidity and
Xavier's treatment of her which enabled Louisa to
keep going through the rest of that traumatic day. It
gave her the energy and drive to make her plans to
leave the castle—and to remain as calm as possible
while she quickly threw a few clothes into a small
suitcase, and checked that her open plane ticket to
London was still viable, tucking it safely away in her
handbag, alongside her new passport.

Knowing that Tante Sophie was due to join some
friends for an early evening game of bridge, she waited
until the chauffeur, Franco—as he'd done in previous
weeks—brought the large limousine around to the
front door of the castle, all ready for Tante's departure,
before going off to have an early supper with his wife,
Rosa.

Louisa never knew how she found the nerve and
resolution to put her hastily assembled plan into action.
But, after stealing quietly out of the castle, it seemed
only a moment or two later that, with her heart
thumping madly in her chest, she was making her way
slowly down the mountain.

Despite feeling almost sick with nerves, Louisa was
quite pleased with her progress, and her apparent
ability to master the powerfully engined, heavy vehicle—when disaster struck.

The setting sun was very low on the horizon, shining
straight into her eyes as she rounded a sharp bend.
Suddenly panic-stricken at seeing a car approaching
very fast, and apparently aimed straight at her, Louisa
quickly turned the wheel to avoid a collision. But, in
the chaotic confusion of the moment, she forgot that

she wasn't driving on an English road, instinctively turning the wheel to the left. She had a blurred impression of a harsh screech of metal on rock, her own cry of terror and a sickening thud, as she was flung forward against the windscreen and knew no more. . .

As through a thick blanket of fog, she was dimly aware of blaring sirens, strange voices, and of being lifted from the wrecked limousine. When Louisa at last regained consciousness, it was to see an unknown man staring down at her with concern. As her eyes slowly came into focus, she saw that he was wearing a white coat.

'We have been worried about you, *madame*. It is good to see that you are awake, at last. How do you feel?' he asked.

'I. . . I think I'm all right,' she muttered woosily, feeling battered and bruised as she tried to remember what had happened. Wincing with pain as she turned her head, to see a nurse standing on the other side of the bed, she slowly realised that she must be in hospital. And then, in an instinctive movement, she placed a hand on her stomach. 'My baby. . .? Is my baby all right?' She gazed anxiously up at the doctor.

'You are pregnant?' He frowned. When she nodded, he quickly gave instructions to the nurse that, unless it was strictly necessary, *madame* was not to be X-rayed.

'You have been very lucky.' He smiled down at Louisa. 'From all accounts, it would seem that you have escaped from the accident with very little injury, other than a slight cut and bruises on your forehead. We will give you a careful examination, of course, but — other than a bad headache — I am quite sure that both you and the baby are well,' he added firmly.

'You're sure the baby will be all right?' she begged him again. 'I couldn't bear. . . I mean, this baby is *very* important to me — it's all I have of my husband!' she cried in distress, helpless tears welling up in her dazed green eyes.

'Be calm, *madame*! I am quite sure there is no need for you to worry. However, to be certain, we will be keeping you in here overnight. Now, I want you to rest,' he told her sternly. 'That is by far the best medicine, for you *and* the baby.'

Time seemed to pass in a haze, as she dozed fitfully, waking every now and then to sip some water, before finally lapsing into a deep sleep.

When she awoke the next morning, suffering from nothing more than a pounding headache, as the doctor had warned, she learned that she'd had a miraculous escape. Luckily, the other driver concerned had not been badly injured, either. Despite the accident— which had clearly been caused by her forgetting that she was not driving on an English road—the other driver, a salesman with a mobile phone, had been able to telephone for assistance, an ambulance promptly arriving to carry them both off to the Hôpital Civil at Corte.

The long day seemed to pass very slowly. Gaining the necessary information from the passport in her handbag, the authorities had contacted the castle, before informing Louisa that she was due to be picked up later that afternoon.

After being dressed in a fresh cotton blouse and skirt, which had apparently been dispatched to the hospital by Tante Sophie, she found herself wearily awaiting the arrival of the elderly woman. Sitting listless in a chair by the window of her hospital room, Louisa was glumly ashamed to have been the cause of so much trouble. Especially for poor Tante Sophie, who'd always been so kind to her, and who didn't deserve all the hassle and worry she must have been caused by this stupid accident. Immersed in despair and misery, she slowly raised her head as a nurse opened the door. A second later, she almost collapsed with shock as the tall figure of Xavier strode into the room!

Feeling quite sick as her stomach gave a sudden nervous lurch, her brain seemed to be a jumbled mass of panic as she stared at him with dazed eyes.

'Well, Louisa?' he drawled blandly. 'It seems that you have caused us all a great deal of worry and concern, hmm?'

But, instead of the cold, harsh tone which she'd instinctively feared, there was nothing in his deep voice or the blank, enigmatic expression on his handsome face to indicate what he was thinking.

Even after the nurse had helped her into the wheel-chair, and she was being pushed down the corridors, accompanied by Xavier's tall figure, he still had said nothing more about the accident. In fact, his continuing silence as she was carefully helped into his low-slung sports car was distinctly unnerving, and as he drove them out of the town there seemed nothing she could do to stop herself shaking like a leaf.

The tense silence in the car seemed to last forever, until Louisa's nerves felt as if they were stretched to breaking-point. Finally she gave a heavy sigh, leaning her sore head back against the seat.

'Why don't you go ahead and say it?' she murmured wearily.

'Why don't I say—what?'

'I suppose something along the lines of "I told you so" would seem to be appropriate,' she muttered bleakly. 'You told me not to drive on the mountains, and you were quite right. I'm sorry to have bashed up the limousine,' she added, with a weary sigh. 'I hope Tante Sophie will forgive me for spoiling her game of bridge, and——'

'*For God's sake*! My aunt's bridge game is the very *least* of my problems at the moment!' he growled angrily, before lapsing into a menacing silence, which she found far more frightening than anything he might say.

Cautiously, she stole a glance through her eyelashes at his stern profile. The arrogant features bore a harsh, strained expression, and there seemed to be dark shadows beneath his eyes as he grimly concentrated on the road before him.

They had been travelling for some time before she realised that they were speeding along a quite unfamiliar route.

'Where are we going?' she demanded, trying to sound stronger than she felt, but not at all sure that she'd succeeded. 'Why aren't we returning to the castle?'

'Because I have decided to take you to my old family home in the Balange — on the north-west coast of the island. It is very quiet and peaceful,' he added firmly as she opened her mouth to protest. 'Besides which, I think that we would both be happier away from the castle, *non*?'

Louisa decided that she was feeling just too tired, exhausted and emotionally drained to care *where* he was taking her. Closing her eyes against the late afternoon sun, she dozed fitfully in the car, until she noticed they were slowing down to turn off the main road. After driving down a long track, Xavier eventually brought the car to a halt outside an old house, surrounded by green lawns and trees, and she realised that they must have arrived at their destination.

'I can manage. I don't need any help,' she muttered as he came around to open the passenger door.

'Don't be such a fool, Louisa!' he growled impatiently. Taking her by surprise, he quickly stooped to gather up her slim figure in his arms, carrying her with ease as he strode swiftly towards the house. At his approach, the large oak front door was thrown wide open, to disclose the plump and beaming figure of a middle-aged woman.

Everything seemed to be happening with such speed that it was difficult for Louisa to have more than a brief impression of the woman, who seemed to bear a strong resemblance to Franco's wife, Rosa.

Cradled in Xavier's strong embrace as he mounted a wide old dark staircase, her vision was filled by his handsome profile. She could see the faint flush on his taut cheekbones beneath the smoothly tanned skin, the rapid beat of a pulse in his firmly clenched jaw. She was suddenly swept by a mad impulse to smooth away the lock of dark curly hair which had fallen over his wide forehead, to press her lips to the corner of his rigidly tense mouth. . .

Before she could give way to such an insane desire, she found herself being lowered down on to the soft mattress of an ancient four-poster bed. It was light years away from the sumptuously draped *lit à la Polanaise* at the castle, but it seemed far more homely and comforting. While Xavier left her for a moment, before returning with a suitcase from the car, she was suddenly overcome by exhaustion, swept by a deep longing to curl up beneath the cosy warmth of the bed's thick, quilted eiderdown.

'It's all right—I can manage!' she protested weakly, as Xavier came over to sit down on the bed beside her, and began to undo the buttons on her blouse.

'May the good lord give me patience!' he ground out savagely. 'If I hear you say "I can manage" just once more—I will *not* be held responsible for my actions! *Tu comprends*?' he demanded.

'Y-Yes. . .' she gasped, shrinking back against the pillows as the sound of his furiously angry voice reverberated loudly around the room. Confused and frightened, she meekly allowed him to remove her clothes, her cheeks flushing hectically as he carefully slipped a fresh, fine lawn nightgown down over her bare shoulders.

'My poor Louisa—you will feel much better after a good sleep,' he murmured softly, his anger clearly having died away as quickly as it had arisen. His hands seemed ineffably gentle as he eased her tired and weary body between the cool linen sheets, which were fragrant with the scent of lavender.

'I. . .I'm sorry to be such a nuisance,' she whispered, as he covered her with the quilt. 'I've caused everyone so much trouble. . .and wrecked your limousine. . .' She was ashamed to feel her eyes filling with weak, helpless tears.

'Hush, *ma chérie*. I don't give a damn about the car—only that you should be alive and well,' he murmured huskily, leaning over to softly brush his mouth over her trembling lips. 'Just relax and go to sleep, hmm? We will have plenty of time to talk tomorrow.'

CHAPTER TWELVE

WHEN Louisa woke up the next morning, it took her some time to remember exactly where she was. And then, as the memory of the previous day flooded back into her mind, she lay staring blindly up at the top of the four-poster bed for a long time.

It must have been the traumatic effect of the car accident which had left her feeling so mentally exhausted yesterday. So weary, and emotionally drained of all feeling, that she hadn't been able to react to the bombshell of Xavier's sudden, dramatic reappearance with anything more than shock and confusion. But now that she'd had the benefit of a long, deep and refreshing sleep, the fog was gradually clearing from her mind, to reveal some brutally hard and unpalatable truths.

Quite how Xavier had so quickly heard about her accident, she had no idea. However, his decision to bring her to this lovely old house — many miles away from the castle — could only mean one thing: a desire for privacy in which to arrange their divorce.

But what else did she expect? she asked herself with a heavy heart. After all, their marriage had never had any real chance of success. What, for her, had been a brief idyll of joy and happiness could now be seen as nothing but a chimera — a pathetic fantasy and delusion, which had quickly proved to have no basis in real life.

Her dismal thoughts were interrupted by a knock on the door, and the entry of the plump and jolly-looking middle-aged woman whom she'd seen so briefly yesterday, bearing a tray of hot coffee and croissants. Beaming at Louisa, she announced that she was Monsier le Comte's housekeeper, Cristina, and if there was anything she could do to make *madame* more comfortable, *madame* had only to ask.

Louisa, who hadn't yet become used to being waited on hand and foot, was thankful for Cristina's help as she gingerly and carefully raised herself up against the pillows. The fleeting impression she'd gained yesterday—of this woman's bearing such a strong resemblance to the housekeeper at the castle—was confirmed as Cristina announced that she was Rosa's older sister.

'Rosa tells me that you are far too thin! So, please eat up your *petit déjeuner*, *madame*, because I have faithfully promised my sister to look after both you—*and* the baby!' she added with a warm smile, before leaving the room.

Although she felt sore and bruised, with an incipient headache beginning to make itself felt at the back of her head, Louisa realised that she was incredibly lucky to have escaped any serious injury in the car accident. Carefully swinging her legs off the bed, she padded slowly across the rugs covering the wide, highly polished oak floorboards, towards the window.

It was a lovely fresh morning. As she gazed out at the long expanse of green lawn, edged by chestnut trees nodding gently in the slight breeze, she could see a village of small houses, perched on the hillside amid sun-lit olive groves, with the blue of the sea in the far distance. As if in a trance, Louisa stared out at the lovely scene, which might have come from an Impressionist painting by Monet or Cézanne, her mind seemingly frozen and refusing to function properly as she tried to think what to do.

One of Neville Frost's favourite phrases floated into her mind. Yes—she really *must* try to 'evaluate the current situation', she told herself grimly. But it was almost impossible to do so, when it seemed as though her whole being was throbbing for the comfort and security of Xavier's strong embrace. How could she hope to concentrate on the problem, when every fibre of her trembling body was aching for his unobtainable love?

But, somehow, Louisa knew that she must try to face the facts of life. And that meant, first and foremost, the acceptance of a harsh and brutal truth: that ever since her arrival in Corsica she'd clearly been living in Cloud-cuckoo-land. She must accept that her marriage was over—before it had even barely begun. And so whether she would have succeeded in her aim of running away, or whether now, here in this house, she and Xavier raked through the cold embers of their marriage made very little difference to the end result.

With a deep sigh, her head throbbing and pounding at the contemplation of the long, lonely life ahead of her, she began listlessly sorting through the contents of the suitcase.

After several cups of strong coffee, and realising that she couldn't stay hiding up here in the bedroom all day, Louisa eventually forced herself to go downstairs. Despite knowing that it was merely a pathetic attempt to keep her courage up, she'd made a determined effort to try to look her best. And thanks to Tante Sophie, who'd clearly not only packed the fresh nightgowns, but also some make-up and a favourite jade-green cotton dress, Louisa felt better able to cope with what was bound to be a deeply distressing situation.

Moving slowly down the stairs, she realised that her confused impressions yesterday had hardly done justice to the lovingly cared for old mansion house, which could just as easily have been found in her native England. She was aware of an entrancing scent of sweet lavender and beeswax polish, her eyes drawn to fine old paintings on the walls, and the gleam of silver jugs and bowls reflected in the highly polished surface of many ancient pieces of rustic furniture, carved from the rich chestnut wood which grew so prolifically on the island. The old velvet curtains were undoubtedly shabby, but the glow of their silky pile, together with the muted colours of the rugs and the mellow gleam from the rich bindings of the old leather-bound books, all combined to add to the warm and comforting atmosphere of the old house.

She was just staring up at a large oil-painting of an eighteenth-century gentleman when she was suddenly startled by the sound of Xavier's voice.

'You are looking at a portrait of Pasquale Paoli, the father of our Corsican nation—and a very great man. That painting is one of my family's proudest possessions.'

Nervously spinning around, Louisa caught her breath as she stared at her husband. A shaft of sunlight from the open doorway was illuminating his tall figure, dressed in a casual pair of trousers and a short-sleeved, open-necked shirt. He looked so impossibly handsome, despite the stern lines of stress and strain about his firmly clenched mouth and jaw, that it was all she could do not to throw herself into his arms.

While Xavier was describing the historic role of Paoli's fight for Corsican independence in the mid-eighteenth century, and his eventual exile and death in England, she found herself struggling against an insane longing to press herself against the strong, hard body standing so close to her own.

'Have you had your breakfast?'

'Yes, I. . .' Louisa gulped, making a desperate effort to try to pull herself together.

'I hope you ate it all? It is important that you keep your strength up, for the baby as well as yourself,' he told her sternly.

The mention of her pregnancy effectively prevented Louisa from saying anything, as he took her arm and led her from the house. Feeling stupidly tongue-tied and awkward, she found herself walking silently beside him across the lawn, past a small grove of eucalyptus trees, towards a vine-covered summer-house, positioned so as to give a view of the hills in the distance.

'It—er—it's a lovely house,' she murmured, tentatively breaking the silence as she turned to look back at the old mansion. 'Did you say it was your family home?'

'Yes. We are supposed to have been descended from a medieval Italian knight, who settled here on his way back from the crusades.' Xavier shrugged his shoulders as they sat down on the bench inside the summer-house. 'That's just an old legend, of course. However,

my ancestors were great landowners here for many
hundreds of years. Unfortunately, they became steadily
poorer as the agricultural economy of this island
declined, and our fortunes hit rock-bottom when my
father died so young, leaving my mother with virtually
nothing but a pittance. However, my roots are here in
this land, and I have always refused to sell the house —
keeping it exactly as it was when I was young, although
it has now become old and shabby. It holds very many
happy memories for me. . .' He sighed and fell silent
for some moments.

Sitting beside him in the cool, dim shade of the
summer-house, Louisa gazed fixedly down at her
hands, bracing herself for the moment when he would
begin to talk about his plans for their divorce.

However, it seemed that Xavier was in no hurry to
begin the discussion, apparently buried in deep thought
as he stared out at the view in front of him. The lengthy
silence seemed to be stretching her nerves to scream-
ing-pitch, becoming almost unbearable as she stole a
quick glance at the tall, remote figure sitting at the
other end of the garden seat.

It was, of course, far too late to try to mend matters
between them. And, after all, what was the point in
even attempting to do so? How could she possibly
begin to explain that her problems had always stemmed
from the fact that he didn't love her?

'Well, Louisa,' he said at last, in a low voice. 'It is
clearly time that we had a long and frank talk together.
Although I confess that I'm not at all sure where to
begin.'

'Please — there's no need to go into any long explanations,' she assured him hurriedly. 'I. . .I really don't
think I can bear it. And, in any case, Désirée has
explained just about everything.'

'Désirée. . .?' He gave a snort of grim anger.
'Désirée knows *nothing*!'

'Well, it seems she does. . .and I can see that it isn't
entirely your fault,' Louisa muttered. 'I mean, I can
understand that you still feel very deeply about your

first wife. I don't suppose you can help it. . .still being in love with her, and——'

'*In love*. . .? With *Georgette*. . .?' Xavier gave a bark of harsh, caustic laughter that grated in her ears. 'Where on earth did you get the *extraordinary* idea that I am supposedly still in love with my dead wife?' he demanded angrily.

Louisa gazed at him in shock and bemusement. 'Well, from Désirée, of course. She said——'

'That woman!' He swore grimly under his breath. 'She has always been nothing but a trouble-maker! Although I suppose I should be grateful to her for telephoning me in Paris two days ago, even if the stupid woman was completely hysterical!'

Louisa frowned and shook her head. 'I really don't understand what you're talking about. . .'

'I was in the middle of a very important board meeting—the reason why I was detained in Paris and did not return to the castle as soon as I had meant to. But when Désirée began screaming down the phone. . . I couldn't understand what she was shouting about, except that it somehow concerned you and the baby. . . I immediately dropped everything and flew straight back to Ajaccio. Only to find that you had nearly killed yourself on the mountain,' he added heavily.

'But she said. . .she said she'd seen you in Paris, and that you'd been talking together about me, on the phone.'

'Nonsense!' His face darkened in anger. 'The only time I saw the woman was when I was having a business meeting—a working dinner with some Japanese clients. She came up to my table at Maxim's and, since we were in the middle of some intricate business, I merely said hello and goodbye. As for my telephoning her—that is a *complete* fabrication!'

Louisa closed her eyes for a moment, her mind in total confusion. 'But she said. . .she *definitely* said that although you'd married me you were still in love with your first wife.'

'For God's sake, Louisa!' he exploded. 'I've never

heard anything so *ridiculous*! How *can* you have believed such stupid nonsense?'

'Do you mean. . .are you saying that you *didn't* love your first wife?'

'Oh, no—not at all.' He sighed, his brief spurt of anger dying away as he turned his head to give her a crooked, twisted smile. 'In fact, on the day of our marriage, I was most definitely head over heels and blindly in love with the girl.'

His quiet words pierced Louisa to the heart. If only she could crawl into a dark hole, to escape from having to listen to Xavier relate his deep love for Georgette. Quivering with pain and anguish, she tightly clasped her arms about her trembling body.

'Oh, yes—I considered myself quite one of the happiest and most fortunate of men. And then, alas, I very quickly discovered that my exquisitely beautiful wife was a greedy, ruthlessly selfish and grasping woman. She'd come from an old, aristocratic family who'd fallen on hard times, and apparently our marriage was designed to restore *her* family's fortunes! In fact, it was only a month after our wedding when she freely admitted that she'd only married me for my money. By that time, I already knew in my heart that I had made a really *terrible* mistake.'

Louisa stared at him, hardly daring to believe her own ears. Was he actually saying that all her unhappiness and jealousy had been totally unnecessary. . .?

Xavier gave a heavy sigh. 'However, what finally killed anything I might have felt for Georgette was the episode regarding our baby.'

Almost light-headed as she felt the hard, painful knot in her stomach beginning to loosen and unwind, Louisa found herself saying, 'I didn't know that you and Georgette had a child. . .?'

'No—we didn't. She quite deliberately arranged to have an abortion, before I even knew she was expecting a baby,' he said in a tight, hard voice. 'She told me that it wasn't at all "chic" to have a baby. And that she was not prepared to have her figure ruined by an unwanted pregnancy!'

'But. . .but, Xavier! Those are the very words you said to me!'

'I know. . .' He shook his head wearily. 'I can only think it must have been because of your deep distress over the baby, the fact that you were so clearly shocked on learning of your pregnancy. But it all suddenly came back to me. I can't really explain. . . I just had this dreadful sense of *déjà vu*. And, of course, with my constant torment. . .the deep feelings of guilt. . .'

He broke off, rising to his feet in agitation, and going over to stand in the open doorway, gazing out at the distant hills.

'For years and years, it seems, I have carried a heavy burden of guilt,' he continued, keeping his back to her as he related the story of his unhappy marriage, and its aftermath.

'I was so desperately unhappy with my wife — totally devastated when she told me that she'd deliberately killed our unborn child — and yet pride prevented me from discussing the matter with anyone. I knew she was seeing other men, I knew she was worthless, but I took my marriage vows very seriously. There was nothing I could do. However, although we remained married in the sight of the world, I eventually gave up trying to make it work. And then. . .then Georgette was killed in that horrific car accident on the mountains. . .' He gave another heavy sigh.

'Oh, Xavier!' Louisa whispered tearfully, her heart wrung by the deep misery and distress in his voice as he recalled his unhappy past.

He slowly turned and came back to sit down beside her. 'It is time I told you the truth,' he said, taking her trembling hands in his. 'And the truth is — that when I heard of Georgette's death I could only feel a deep sense of relief. It was a terrible thing, that I could feel no grief. . .to be glad that she was dead. I have had to live with it all these years. . .years of shame and self-disgust that I could be so hard, so callous. You cannot condemn me more than I do myself. The only way I have been able to cope with the burden, and with the memory of my wretchedly unhappy marriage, has been to immerse myself in work—to concentrate on making money. After all,' he added with a harsh bark of bitter, caustic laughter, 'I told myself that, while I may have failed at everything else in life, at least I am *very* successful at making money, *non*?'

Louisa could have wept for the proud, arrogant man. 'Please, Xavier—you mustn't torture yourself like this,' she murmured helplessly.

'Ah—but then, you see, after so many unhappy years, there suddenly burst into my dreary life—or, to be exact, into my office in Ajaccio—a quite extraordinary English girl, with red-gold hair and startled green eyes that reminded me of a highly strung, nervous racehorse. She was also, I may say, extremely aggressive, not to say outrageously rude——'

'What nonsense!' Louisa exclaimed. '*You* were the one who was so rude!'

'And *so* argumentative! Besides which, she was *definitely* not the type of woman to whom I was normally attracted. And yet. . .I found myself realising that life was suddenly worth living, after all. It was both wonderful and terrifying—at one and the same time!'

'Well, I was certainly terrified of *you*,' she sighed unhappily. 'Especially when you kept on demanding that my brother marry Marie-Thérèse!'

'Well, yes, I will confess that I was wrong. I'm afraid that I did go slightly over the top about Marie-Thérèse. You see, I had got so used to thinking of my niece as a young girl, whose virtue must be protected. And then, quite suddenly, it seemed that she had become a young woman, skipping out of the house at all hours of the night. . . I was *very* worried and concerned about her.'

'Well, at least you're allowing her to lead her own life now—which has to be right. But really and truly, Xavier, you do seem to have a most extraordinary attitude to women. Look at the way you refused to do business with me just because I was a female!'

'Oh, no, *ma petite*. I had you removed from that job for one reason and one reason only. I could not possibly do business with a girl when I was in the process of falling very deeply in love with her. So of course the job had to go.' He gave an arrogant, dismissive wave of his hand. 'However——'

'*What*?' Louisa exclaimed, not at all sure that she'd heard him correctly. 'Do you really mean. . .that you really do——?'

'Please—just let me finish what I have to say.' Xavier raised an imperious hand. 'Which is that I had a long talk with the doctor at the hospital in Corte. He told me how worried you were about losing the baby—how anxious you were that it should come to no harm.

'My darling Louisa!' he continued doggedly as she tried to interrupt. 'I don't know how to find sufficient words of deep apology—both for behaving so crassly when you first heard of your pregnancy, and then for putting you through such torment of spirit. I don't understand how I could have allowed myself to be so swamped by dark, hideous memories of the past. Or how I could treat you so badly. I know. . .well, in fact I'm quite certain that you won't ever really be able to forgive me. But I love you so much, *ma belle*—with all my heart—and for the sake of the child. . .? I cannot bear the thought of my son growing up, as I had to do, without a father's love. And although I forced you into marriage with me by the deliberate use of the strong sexual attraction we felt to each other, I would like us to stay together. . .' He brushed an agitated, shaking hand roughly through his hair, his English breaking down beneath the stress of his emotion. 'I know. . . I understand that you cannot love me, but maybe in time——?'

'*Oh, for goodness' sake!*' Louisa cried, before happily throwing her arms about his neck. 'You stupid, *stupid* man! Can't you see that I love you with all my heart? I fell madly in love with you, practically the first time we met. The truth is—I thought that you didn't love *me*!'

He looked at her in astonishment. 'Not love you? But why else would I have bought a controlling share in an English firm, except to keep that boring young man, Neville Frost, well away from my lovely wife?' he growled with impatience, before seizing her in his arms and giving her a long, lingering and deeply satisfying kiss.

'And you really *are* happy about the baby?' Louisa whispered, when she'd managed to regain her breath.

'How can you doubt it?' he murmured, fervently kissing her again.

'Well. . .Neville is certainly happy running the business,' Louisa told him breathlessly, as she lay clasped in his embrace. 'But what about all *your* old girlfriends? And don't try and tell me that you've been as pure as the driven snow—because I won't believe you! I can still remember your very first, *amazingly* arrogant words,' she added darkly. 'How did it go. . .? "I am quite accustomed to being chased by women". . .?'

'Ah—*ma chérie*!' he protested, his cheeks flushing slightly beneath the smooth tan. 'It is *very* unfair of you to remember such a stupid statement.' He shook his dark head. 'What an arrogant fool I must have seemed!'

'Well, actually. . .' She grinned. 'If it makes you feel any better, I'm quite willing to confess that I thought you were just about the best-looking, sexiest man I'd ever seen! On the other hand—and just to keep your feet on the ground, my darling Xavier—I'd also never come across anyone *quite* so arrogant in my whole life! And as for all that business about "honour" and "revenge". . .!'

'Ah, *ma belle*—surely you must see that love has now taken a fine revenge on me? And I can faithfully assure you that ever since the first moment we met there has *never* been anyone else in my life. Nor will there ever be,' he vowed softly, sealing his words with a kiss of mounting passion that embodied a firm promise and total commitment.

Welcome to Europe

CORSICA — 'a mountain in the sea'

Now officially a *département* of France, Corsica combines the attractions of that country with many claims of its own. The French call it *'ile de beauté'*, and the visitor can expect to find soaring peaks, mysterious deep gorges, foaming torrents and brooding forests of pines; or, alternatively, flowery meadows, farms, olive groves and orchards. A history of bloody vendetta and feud, foreign occupation and fights for independence, in common with its very near neighbour Sardinia, which it almost touches, give it a vibrant sense of identity which lives on today after the battles have ceased.

THE ROMANTIC PAST

Very little was written about Corsica in ancient times, though one writer recorded that two sons of Hercules, Sardus and Kyrnos, conquered and settled Sardinia and Corsica respectively. We know, however, that there were people in Corsica as early as 8000 years ago. A human skeleton unearthed at l'Araguina-Sennola has been dated back to 6750 BC. Since then, the islands have been occupied and administrated by Greeks, Carthaginians, Romans, Vandals, Ostragoths, Byzantines, Saracens, Pisans and Genoese. The island's only period of independence was between 1755 and 1769, when **Pasquale**

Paoli, a name you will surely hear often on a visit to Corsica, was elected General of the nation; this was good enough for everyone except the Genoese, who ceded Corsica to France by the Treaty of Versailles in 1768, and the French army crushed Paoli's troops.

The continual battles for independence mean that the Corsican people are renowned for having a highly developed sense of patriotism and courage, a courage which in more recent decades has been an advantage to the French nation. Corsica is famous for being the birthplace of Napoléon Bonaparte; then in World War I the island lost 40,000 men, more than any other French *département*. And in the Second World War the dense white-flowered *maquis* brushwood which hid Corsican bandits and victims of vendetta gave its name to the French Resistance movement.

The symbol of Corsica is the '**Moor's Head**', though no one knows for certain what it represents. The most romantic legend says it is the head of a Moorish king who tried to abduct a Corsican girl but was slain by her fiancé. Originally the head was blindfolded, but Pasquale Paoli raised the blindfold during the War of Independence as a symbol of the awakening of the Corsican people.

Most of the folklore of the island is rooted in the darkness and violence of its turbulent past. Children are taught to fear the *streghi*, witches who sneak into the house at night to suck babies' blood, and the *acciatori*, who lurk in the dark to chop off the heads of unwary travellers! But feuds and vendettas make good stories, and have inspired writers such as Prosper Mérimée and Alexandre Dumas. They also led to the strong culture of folk song which still exists today.

THE ROMANTIC PRESENT — pastimes for lovers. . .

The first thing that will strike you as you step off your boat or aeroplane on to Corsica's shores will be its overwhelming scent, which gives it the name 'the scented isle'. Napoléon said, 'I would recognise Corsica with my eyes closed from its perfume alone.' Apart from the distinctive fragrance of the *maquis*, the island is alive throughout the year with the bright colours of numerous exotic flowers and countless herbs.

A good place to begin to get to know Corsica would be its capital, **Ajaccio**. Founded in 1492, the year when Christopher Columbus — whom some claim not to be Genoese at all, but a Corsican from Calvi — discovered America, this bustling and lively town has an excellent sandy beach as well as many shops and a variety of nightlife. The fact that it is the birthplace of Napoléon Bonaparte is evident from the various statues of him dotted around the town. The **Musée Fesch** is worth a visit for its collection of early Italian paintings, and if you happen to be in the town on June 2nd don't miss the religious procession through the town in honour of St Erasmus, patron saint of fishermen.

On the southern tip of the island is the picturesque harbour town of **Bonifacio**, a network of tiny cobbled streets lined with craft shops and cafés. According to Homer's *Odyssey*, Odysseus stopped here for shelter and rest just as many tourists do today in its harbour area tucked into a deep cleft between limestone cliffs. The town was a pirate stronghold in the 9th century, and the Genoese took control of it only by surprising the pirates when they were drunk at a wedding feast. Visit the **'King of Aragon's Staircase'**: 187 steps carved in the rockface up from the sea. The staircase is said to have been cut in a single night in 1420 by Aragonese soldiers!

One of the most picturesque towns in the north of the island is **Centuri-Port** on Cap Corse. Compared to other towns it is one of the most unspoilt, and oozes with charm with its green-tiled roofs, miniature harbour and small sandy beach.

There are many other fascinating and beautiful resorts around the phenomenally varied 1000-mile coastline. But it is if you venture into the central island area that you get a sense of the turbulent past of vendettas and battles. The largest central town is **Corte**, highly atmospheric with its narrow streets, dark façades and silent stone stairways. In its main square, **Place Gaffori**, there is a statue of General Gaffori and behind it the house he lived in, pitted with bullet marks from the time of the Corsican freedom struggle. The story is told that when the general's house was being besieged by the Genoese in 1750, he was away, but his wife Faustina persuaded the people to hold out under the siege by waving a lighted torch over a barrel of gunpowder. Eventually Gaffori arrived and the siege was lifted.

There are two fountains in the streets off Cours Paoli in Corte. One, called the *Douze Cailloux*, is so named because it is said that it's so cold that you can only remove twelve pebbles before your hand freezes!

And, for the romantic at heart, surely you must fit in a pilgrimage to **Montemaggiore**—the birthplace of the mother of the greatest lover of all, Don Juan!

If all this sightseeing has made you hungry, you will find plenty of Corsican specialities that are worth picking out from among the usual tourist fare. Corsican food includes game in season, chestnuts used in both sweet and savoury dishes, cheese made from sheep or goat's milk, pâté made from blackbirds and pigeons, and a wide variety of pork products. Look out for *saliccio*, a peppery spiced sausage or *figatelli*, another kind of sausage made from black smoked pork, **prisuttu** ham (similar to the Italian *prosciutto*) or the soft **brocciu** cheese made of a mixture of whey and whole milk, used in cooking or eaten as a dessert cheese. The more adventurous among you might like to try some local dishes like **ziminu**, a kind of *bouillabaisse* (fish soup) with croutons and grated hard cheese; **tianu de cignale**, a wild boar hotpot with onions, garlic and potatoes; *pâté de merle*, a blackbird pâté seasoned with local myrtle; *bianchetti*, a local fried whitebait, or even *oursins*—sea-urchins! Whatever dishes you choose, one distinctive feature will be the skilful blending of the many available local herbs—thyme, fennel, myrtle, borage, juniper, rosemary, mint, basil and sage, to name but a few.

To drink with your meal there are some delicious local **wines**. White wine is relatively rare, the main one being **Côteaux du Cap Corse** from the north. Red wines come from the coast around Ajaccio, but the wine most commonly drunk with meals on Corsica is rosé. And after you've eaten your fill, have a nightcap of *cédratine*, a local liqueur made from lemons.

And finally, everyone wants to take home something to keep alive the memories of the wonderful holiday you're bound to have. Wood carving is the main handicraft native to Corsica, but you can also buy pottery, enamel, embroidery and mosaic work, coral brooches and *art galtique*—pictures made of pebbles or small pieces of wood. Look out for the label 'Casa di l'Artigiani' as a guarantee of quality. You could also take home some of the local Roquefort cheese or fragrant honey, or, if your holiday romance has been inspired by the haunting music of the isle, it is possible to buy recordings of the folk songs to bring back 'that loving feeling'.

DID YOU KNOW THAT. . .?

* Corsica is the **fourth largest island** in the Mediterranean, after Sicily, Sardinia and Cyprus. It measures 183 km by 83 km, and its total area is about 8720 km sq, or 3367 square miles.

* French is universally spoken, but the **Corsican language**, closer to Italian than French, flourishes in much the same way as does Welsh in Britain.

* about one-fifth of the total land surface is **forested**.

* the island is divided into two parts, '*En deça-des-Monts*' (the north and east) and '*Au delà-des-Monts*' (the south and west), which translates as 'this side of the mountains' and 'that side of the mountains'.

* the island's natural resources include asbestos, green slate and marble, but transport costs to the mainland are very high. The island's main **exports** are honey, liqueur and Roquefort cheese and tobacco.

* to say 'I love you' in Corsica you say, '*Je t'aime.*'

LOOK OUT FOR TWO TITLES EVERY MONTH IN OUR SERIES OF EUROPEAN ROMANCES:

A RECKLESS ATTRACTION: Kay Thorpe (Norway)
Kirstan had come to Norway to pour oil on troubled family waters. But would disturbingly attractive Terje Bruland allow her to succeed, when he seemed determined to think the worst of her?

A TOUCH OF APHRODITE: Joanna Mansell (Cyprus)
Emily could hardly believe her luck when she inherited a hotel in Cyprus. The trouble was, Nikolaos Konstantin strongly disapproved—and made his displeasure abundantly clear!

LAIR OF THE DRAGON: Catherine George (Wales)
Naomi hated deceiving Bran Lllewelyn by posing as his secretary. But if she revealed her deception, how could she hang on to his love?

THE DARK EDGE OF LOVE: Sara Wood (Madeira)
Ellen was sure she hated arrogant Adden de Torre. So why did passion flare so strongly between them? Could their feelings for each other be more complicated?

FREE

GOLD PLATED BRACELET

MILLS & BOON

NEW LOOK MILLS & BOON ROMANCES

A few months ago we introduced new look covers on our Romance series and we'd like to hear just how much you like them.

Please spare a few minutes to answer the questions below and we will send you a **FREE** Mills & Boon novel as a thank you. Just send the completed questionnaire back to us today - **NO STAMP NEEDED.**

Don't forget to fill in your name and address, so that we know where to send your **FREE** book!

Please tick the appropriate box to indicate your answers. ☑

1. **For how long have you been a Mills & Boon Romance reader?**
   Since the new covers ☐   1 to 2 years ☐   6 to 10 years ☐
   Less than 1 year ☐   3 to 5 years ☐   Over 10 years ☐

2. **How frequently do you read Mills & Boon Romances?**
   Every Month ☐   Every 2 to 3 Months ☐   Less Often ☐

3. **From where do you usually obtain your Romances?**
   Mills & Boon Reader Service ☐   Supermarket ☐
   W H Smith/John Menzies/Other Newsagent ☐
   Boots/Woolworths/Department Store ☐
   Other (please specify:)_____

4. **Please let us know how much you like the new covers:**

Like very much ☐   Don't like very much ☐

Like quite a lot ☐   Don't like at all ☐

5. **What do you like most about the design of the covers?** _____

_____

_____

6. **What do you like least about the design of the covers?** _____

_____

_____

7. **Do you have any additional comments you'd like to make about our new look Romances?** _____

_____

_____

8. **Do you read any other Mills & Boon series? (Please tick each series you read).**

Love on Call (Medical Romances) ☐   Temptation ☐

Legacy of Love (Masquerade) ☐   Duet ☐

Favourites (Best Sellers) ☐   Don't read any others ☐

9. **Are you a Reader Service subscriber?**

Yes ☐   No ☐

If Yes, what is your subscriber number? _____

10. **What is your age group?**

16-24 ☐   25-34 ☐   35-44 ☐   45-54 ☐   55-64 ☐   65+ ☐

THANK YOU FOR YOUR HELP

✉   Please send your completed questionnaire to: ✉

**Mills & Boon Reader Service, FREEPOST,
P O Box 236, Croydon, Surrey CR9 9EL**

NO STAMP NEEDED

Ms/Mrs/Miss/Mr: _____ NR

Address: _____

_____

_____ Postcode: _____

You may be mailed with offers from other reputable companies as a result of this
application. Please tick box if you would prefer not to receive such offers. ☐
One application per household.

mps
*MAILING
PREFERENCE
SERVICE*

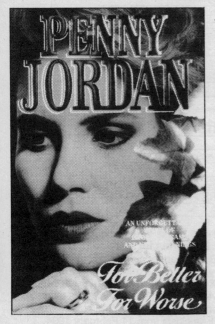

Next Month's Romances

Each month you can choose from a wide variety of romance with Mills & Boon. Below are the new titles to look out for next month, why not ask either Mills & Boon Reader Service or your Newsagent to reserve you a copy of the titles you want to buy – just tick the titles you would like and either post to Reader Service or take it to any Newsagent and ask them to order your books.

Please save me the following titles:	Please tick	√
HEART-THROB FOR HIRE	Miranda Lee	
A SECRET REBELLION	Anne Mather	
THE CRUELLEST LIE	Susan Napier	
THE AWAKENED HEART	Betty Neels	
ITALIAN INVADER	Jessica Steele	
A RECKLESS ATTRACTION	Kay Thorpe	
BITTER HONEY	Helen Brooks	
THE POWER OF LOVE	Rosemary Hammond	
MASTER OF DECEIT	Susanne McCarthy	
THE TOUCH OF APHRODITE	Joanna Mansell	
POSSESSED BY LOVE	Natalie Fox	
GOLDEN MISTRESS	Angela Wells	
NOT FOR LOVE	Pamela Hatton	
SHATTERED MIRROR	Kate Walker	
A MOST CONVENIENT MARRIAGE	Suzanne Carey	
TEMPORARY MEASURES	Leigh Michaels	

If you would like to order these books in addition to your regular subscription from Mills & Boon Reader Service please send £1.80 per title to: Mills & Boon Reader Service, Freepost, P.O. Box 236, Croydon, Surrey, CR9 9EL, quote your Subscriber No:.................................... (If applicable) and complete the name and address details below. Alternatively, these books are available from many local Newsagents including W.H.Smith, J.Menzies, Martins and other paperback stockists from 11 February 1994.

Name:...

Address:...

....Post Code:...........................

To Retailer: If you would like to stock M&B books please contact your regular book/magazine wholesaler for details.

You may be mailed with offers from other reputable companies as a result of this application. If you would rather not take advantage of these opportunities please tick box ☐